from *OUTCAST BREED*

HAND TO HAND

"I've come to ask a question, and I'll have your answer," said Cameron. "I'll have it...if I have to tear it out of your throat."

Harmody did not walk around the table. He brushed it aside with a light gesture, and all the dishes on it made a clattering.

"You'll tear it out of me?" he said softly, and then he lunged for Cameron.

Up there in the mountain camps, patiently, with fists bare, Mark Wayland had taught his foster son something of the white man's art of self-defense. Cameron used the lessons now. He had no hope of winning; he only hoped that he might prove himself a man. Speed of foot shifted him aside from the first rush. He hit Harmody three times on the side of the jaw as the big target rushed past. It was like hitting a great timber with sacking wrapped over it.

Harmody stopped his rush, turned. He pulled a gun and tossed it aside. "I'm gonna kill you," he said through his teeth, "but I don't want tools to do the job."

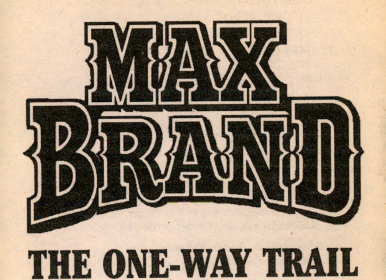

THE ONE-WAY TRAIL

LEISURE BOOKS   NEW YORK CITY

A LEISURE BOOK®

April 1998

Published by special arrangement with
Golden West Literary Agency.

Dorchester Publishing Co., Inc.
276 Fifth Avenue
New York, NY 10001

ISBN 0-8439-4379-3

THE ONE-WAY TRAIL

TABLE OF CONTENTS

FORGOTTEN TREASURE

Forgotten Treasure

The texts used for this and the other short novels appearing in the book are based on a concordance between the author's own typescripts and the versions that first appeared in magazines. The reason for this is two-fold. Frequently texts appearing in magazines had to be cut in order to fit in the space allotted, or upon occasion editorial intervention occurred for a variety of reasons that ultimately corrupted the text. "Forgotten Treasure" was first published in Street & Smith's *Western Story* magazine in the issue dated November 19, 1927. A slightly abridged version of this story read by Barry Corbin was subsequently issued by Audio Renaissance.

Chapter One
Quince Against Dikkon

In the beginning, every Quince was fair of hair, and every Dikkon was dark. Every Quince was tall and broad, and every Dikkon was narrow and small. Every Quince had eyes of green. Every Dikkon had eyes of black. He who had made them so differently set down the families side by side in the mountains of Kentucky.

War, of course, followed and, though the Quinces were bigger and wider and correspondingly stronger, they simply offered a fairer target to the guns of the Dikkons. Finally, a scattered handful of the fair-haired giants packed their belongings and started for the far West. On the way a cruel band of Dikkons swept down upon them and harried them so dreadfully that, in the end, only two small families gained their distant goal.

But even these were not left in peace, for fate led the Dikkons in numbers to the same spot, and the feud began again. At last the name of Quince was reduced to a single man, and that man was outlawed. He married and left a son behind him when five of the Dikkons cornered him in a nest of rocks and paid three lives for his one. It was considered that the price was small, for the more the Quinces were reduced in number, the greater became their strength. Now that this dangerous father was dead, it only remained to comb the mountains and find the boy who lurked somewhere among them. He was but twelve years old, and therefore, when he was found, the last of the viper breed would be wiped out. So they searched for young Barney Quince. Twice they found his bullets, but they did not find him.

He eluded them, and again and again he dodged their searchers. However, the game became so hot that he was forced to leave that district. For three years he disappeared from the Dikkon ken, and their tribe increased and flourished. They nearly owned the rich town of Adare with all the valleys for farming and the highlands for grazing which lay around it. The Dikkons, and those who had married into the clan, dominated this region. They controlled the county, elected the officials, and above all saw that the dignity of sheriff constantly should be vested in a person of the right Dikkon lineage.

Then in his sixteenth year Barney Quince came back and fell upon them like a plague. Their champions rode out against him and came back with weary horses and some empty saddles, but they could not get Barney. They might cut him with their bullets, but they could not cut him to the quick!

He looked upon as his perquisite all that the Dikkons had. If he needed money, it was always a Dikkon he robbed. If he were lacking a swift horse, it was from the Dikkon herds that he cut out the best and the strongest. If he wished for meat, a Dikkon beef or a Dikkon mutton was his victim. All of this he did with the price mounting upon his head but his heart free from the sense of guilt for, it was apparent, he had been nurtured deeply in the lore of the Quince family. His mother had lived long enough to teach him all the past, poisoned with her bitter tongue. So he preyed upon the Dikkons with the subtlety of a desperado and the boldness of an honest man. His known boast was that never a man had fallen before him except one who bore the name of Dikkon, never a penny of money had been taken at the point of a gun except money made by a Dikkon, and never a morsel of food would pass his lips except what he robbed from the Dikkons. He scorned to labor on his own behalf and swore, so that all should know his resolution, all that fed and clothed him should be reaped in a broad and rich harvest from the possessions of his hereditary foes.

For ten dreadful years he was a scourge upon the backs of the Dikkons. They hushed their children at night with his name, and every young Dikkon grew into manhood with a single glorious goal before him—to find and destroy Barney Quince!

One question was asked repeatedly by the clan: had Barney Quince married? No, not yet! Therefore, there was no son and heir to his name and his terrors. The Dikkons might not capture him, but at least they drove him here and there like a swiftly glancing shuttle through the mountains and the valleys so that he could not mate. If they could not take him with their net, at least the peril would vanish with him. Yet others said that he knew this well and would choose his own good time to marry. Before he died surely another of his name would be riding and destroying as he had ridden and destroyed.

This was not merely an occasional theme with the Dikkons, but it mingled bitterly with the bread of every meal that was eaten in the town of Adare. The sun never rose upon their rich valleys, their standing crops, their flocks, and their herds without bringing the thought of Barney Quince coldly upon their hearts.

Consider, then, what horror, wonder, joy, and disbelief were mingled in the souls of the clansmen when, as they sat at their supper tables one evening with the rose of the sunset time beyond their windows, they heard a startled rumor that Barney Quince had come down into the town itself. They rushed out— all the men. The women and the children cowered behind. The armed men, resolute and stern—for when was a Dikkon a coward?—formed a solid van with rifles ready, and then they saw the strangest sight that ever dawned upon their eyes.

For a tall man was walking lightly down the central street along which their houses faced and behind him stepped a magnificent horse, a gray that glimmered brightly in the rose of the evening. They knew the horse, and they knew the man. When it was a magnificent three-year-old, the hope and the pride of Harvey Dikkon, the colt had been stolen from him by the marauder, and for three years now it had served to whisk the evil doer away from his pursuers. That was the gray and before him was Barney Quince, with his long yellow hair shining as it had shone many a time before, blinding the eyes of the Dikkon clansmen. But at the back of his head it was stained and clotted with blood. That blood, and his gay and careless manner as he descended into the town of his enemies, made his coming something that chilled their very souls, because it was a ghostly thing beyond human understanding.

It was doubtless this sense of the unearthly that caused many a rifle, raised to cover him, to fall slowly again, while the gunmen gaped and shook their heads. When he came to the very center of the village, old Ned Dikkon, with a cry, started out into the roadway and brought his rifle to his shoulder.

There was no doubt in his mind. As for a sense of ghostliness in this proceeding, he was familiar with the sad touch of the other world, for his two strong sons had been taken from him, his two gallant boys who stood in the very forefront of the clan for manliness and skill in all that makes a Western rider formidable and famous. They had been taken from him, and there came the man who had stopped their lives—both in one sudden battle of an August afternoon where the trail turns on the gray shoulder of Mount Forrest.

He shouted: "Barney Quince, think of Pete and Charlie Dikkon that you murdered!" He pressed his steady finger slowly around the trigger.

That bullet would have found the heart of Barney Quince without doubt, but Oliver Dikkon, when he saw his older brother start out, rifle in hand, ran after him and came in time to thrust the weapon aside and then wrest it from his grasp.

"Man, man!" he called. "You wouldn't do a murder?"

That broke the spell. A flood of excited men bound the

hands of Barney Quince—those terrible hands which now submitted passively—and they led him to the nearest house which, by chance, was the house of Oliver Dikkon.

It was an excited crowd, and savage voices began to rise in it after the first shock of the surprise had worn away. Oliver Dikkon took control, not only because he was one of the head men in the clan, but because he now could exert a doubled authority as the owner of the house in which they were crowded. He called together the half-dozen recognized leaders of his people. The rest, though sullenly and ill at ease, departed from the dwelling and gathered in the front garden, overflowing into the street.

They did not leave but remained there leaning on their guns. Behind them came the children swarming, and anxious mothers after them telling them in shrill voices to come home again, for where Barney Quince was, there was peril. It was hopeless to try to convince them, however. They swarmed out as they would have swarmed to see the giant Jack killed in the story, filled with fear but also filled with expectant delight.

In the meantime the grim voices among the men were raised now and again. There was not one among them who had not had a father, a brother, a son, a cousin destroyed either by this man or by his hardly less terrible father. There were none who had not ridden, at one time or another, upon his trail. There were men who were scarred by his bullets. There was gigantic Ben Dikkon, for instance, who had closed with the outlaw in single combat on one heroic and never-to-be-forgotten day when he had been left for dead. Now the scars of that dreadful fight were on his body and seamed his face. He towered above the rest of the smaller, dark-faced clansmen, and he alone said nothing, but his set jaw and his narrowed eyes told nonetheless plainly what stirred in his mind.

The others looked at him. Having met the destroyer and lived to tell the tale, he seemed to them like some primeval force, greater than other men, half god-like. They would have welcomed speech from him, but speech there was none. So silence gradually settled over the entire assemblage. Even the children were quiet. Anxious eyes looked up and noted that clouds were gathering heavily across the face of the sun, and a wind cold as night blew down from the upper mountains. Some great event, they knew, was about to come to pass, and gloomily they felt that it did not bode well for the clan of Dikkon.

Chapter Two
Quince Before Dikkon

Within the house they sat in a duly ordered semicircle. At its right tip was Randolph Dikkon whose beard had been white for twenty years. Next to him was Eustace Dikkon, almost as old as Randolph but who, instead of turning white, had remained gray and, instead of withering, had merely shrunk a little and grown harder and harder. Little Henry Dikkon, on Eustace's left, owned a farm in Windale Valley and was prosperous enough for that alone to account for his place on the governing committee. John, beside Henry, had been educated in an eastern university and, growing soft in professional life as a lawyer, he alone graced Adare with a frock coat and a gold chain looped across his increasing stomach. Oliver had his place in this high body, well earned whether as a fighting man, or a shrewd councilor, or as the proprietor of the lumber mill which, on the river just above the town, harnessed the stream and made it do his bidding. Last of all was Martin Glanvil. He had married into the clan and was the first of a foreign name ever to sit in this august assemblage and, therefore, despite his advanced years, he ever had the seat most to the left from the acknowledged master of the Dikkons. He was looked upon, to a degree, as an interloper, but the strength of his broad and patient mind had been tested often, and never had he been found wanting.

So the six wise men sat together and focused their grim attention upon the last of their hereditary enemies. He who alone stood between them and a permanent peace was now helpless in their hands. A cloth was tied around Quince's head for Lou—Louise Dikkon, the daughter of Oliver and the woman of the house—had washed away the blood and found a ghastly wound ridged in his skull. This she had dressed, and now close to the fire which burned on the broad hearth she watched observantly.

"He's had his head broken by a fall," she told them, "and his wits are gone. If you do anything to him, you've done something worse than the murder of a baby."

Eustace Dikkon parted his hard lips. "I remember the story of how the Quinces came down on the house of Jerry Dikkon in Kentucky and murdered the men, then locked the doors and let the women and the children burn. There was a couple of babies inside, I've heard tell."

He expanded his thin, flinty hands toward the distant blaze and rubbed them slowly together, but warmth was something he never would get into his flesh or into his heart.

"What's been done before by man or woman against the Dikkons ain't of account here and now," pronounced Randolph, his hand buried in his beard, "but only what's been done by this here man before us. Barney Quince, you stand up and answer what's asked of you."

The prisoner, when he heard his name, looked up with a pleasant smile which made his handsome face actually beautiful for an instant. But then the light went out of his face, and he remained for a moment with lifted eyes, staring past the heads of the circle as if into some vast distance.

"You see!" said Lou Dikkon, "he don't know a thing. You'd better put him to bed . . . and hang him when he gets his senses back."

"Woman," said Randolph, "leave the room!"

She could not argue against such resistless authority, but for an instant she lingered beside the prisoner and dropped her hand upon his great shoulder.

"He's done his killings," she said, "but he's never fought foul. He's never shot from behind. He's never been a snake in the dark. Dad, you won't let 'em murder this poor half-wit?''

Thunderous silence greeted this appeal, and she shrank from the room, only pausing at the door to cast back a single earnest glance at the big man who sat before the fire with its light glimmering through his long golden hair and touching on the sea-green of his eyes.

Still the silence held. Then the hard lips of Eustace parted again. "Out on my place," he said coldly, "I halter-break the fillies as well as the colts."

Oliver colored under this rebuke, but he made no answer. Old Randolph brought the talk back to its proper subject.

"I've called on you to stand up here, Barney Quince. You hear me talk?"

There was no reply. Barney Quince yawned broadly, touched the back of his head as though it had been stabbed by a pain, and almost instantly fell into a deep study over a cricket that was crawling across the floor toward the heat of the fire.

At this, Randolph said: "He don't answer. What's to be done?"

John Dikkon felt the eyes of the others turning toward him. He expanded a little. One hand he hooked in his massive golden chain. The other hand he laid upon his smooth knee. He depressed his chin a little and said: "In such a case one might proceed by considering silence an affirmation. Threaten him, therefore, that you will proceed in that manner."

"John," said the chairman, "I reckon that you know what this Barney Quince is said to have done. You open up and ask him, all lawyer-like, if you please."

John stood at once. He took a position in front of the captive and, thrusting one hand behind his back, he made the tail of his frock coat stand out like the tail of a rooster. Then, leaning a little, he waved a fat forefinger like a club above the bent head of Barney Quince.

"You, Barney Quince," said the lawyer, "standing before

this bar for judgment and in your contumacy refusing to answer the questions justly put to you and yet being subject justly to its authority, are hereby declared to have returned an affirmative answer to those questions to which you return no answer except silence. Hear me and reply if you have anything to say against this judgment.''

The captive, during the latter part of this little oration, had listened to the speech with a sort of mild wonder, raising his head and regarding the orator with a wandering attention. But now he chuckled softly and, leaning forward, he picked up the cricket and placed it farther from the fire and in the long hair of a bearskin rug—a skin which Oliver Dikkon himself had brought home after a desperate battle with the original wearer.

John Dikkon turned and bowed to the reverend head of the court. ''The prisoner returns no answer and thereby accepts the condition,'' he declared. ''Shall I proceed with the examination?''

''D'you know what you're talkin' about, John?'' asked old Randolph.

''Sir,'' said the lawyer, ''you forget that I am a Dikkon. No man is more familiar with the outrages which are attached to the name of this man.''

''Go on then.''

The lawyer returned to the charge. Again his fat forefinger impended in the air. ''At the tender age of twelve years,'' he said, ''an age when most men are children and unacquainted with the dreadful profession of arms, did you not, when three honorable gentlemen of the name of Dikkon were riding through the mountains, willfully assault them with intent to kill, actually shooting one horse from beneath the person of William Dikkon and striking Harry Dikkon through the shoulder, so that from that day until his death he never had proper use of the afflicted limb?''

''Go on,'' said Randolph, ''you got a good memory, John, but just leave out the age of him when you talk about what he's done to us!''

There was an affirmative stir in the court. Barney Quince was still rapt with the cricket.

"The prisoner returns silence," said the lawyer, "and thereby admits the charge of willfully and feloniously assaulting the persons of three men, killing a horse, and seriously wounding one man. A serious charge!" affirmed John Dikkon. He went on: "Did you not, just three months later, in the middle of the night when two men entered your room in a hostelry known as Larkin's Luck, at a crossroads between Elkhead and Lewis's Crossing, willfully and with malice aforethought, with intent to destroy and take the lives of those two men . . . did you not, Barney Quince, with a gun in either hand attack them, shooting Gerald Dikkon through the hip and neck, so that he lay for months near to death. And did you not at the same time shoot Lawrence Dikkon through the head and through the body, so that he did instantly fall down dead in that room? Answer . . . on the peril of your life!"

The prisoner did not stir, and something between a groan and a growl was heard from the six judges.

"The prisoner returns no answer, and by the agreement already entered into with him," said the man of the law, "this silence is accepted as an acknowledgment of the willful assault upon and murder of Lawrence Dikkon, together with the willful and malicious attack upon and the vital wounding of Gerald Dikkon." He made a little pause then continued: "Three years elapsed and then, on a December night, did you not, Barney Quince, descend from the mountains and raid the ranch of Rathbone Dikkon, taking from him forcibly and at the point of a gun two horses as well as a whole pack of guns, ammunition, and food of various kinds, being all that was in the larder of the said Rathbone Dikkon? And when he with his two sons pursued you, did you not attack the three and willfully and with malice aforethought, with intent to slay, fire upon them, wounding Rathbone Dikkon through the right arm and taking the life of Jerome Dikkon, his eldest son?"

He turned to the court.

"The prisoner remains silent," said the lawyer, "and thereby he pleads guilty to the second charge of having taken the life of a good and law-abiding American citizen, by name Jerome Dikkon, who had acted merely in defense of his just legal rights."

He made another pause and was raising his fateful right hand once more for fresh accusation, when the sharp and brisk voice of Henry Dikkon broke in: "I dunno that there's any use asking the rest of the list, unless you can hang a man higher for fifteen murders than you can for two. Suppose that we start figuring what we're gonna do with this gent?"

The mention of the round number of actual deaths among the clan which had occurred because of this man caused a shudder to pass through the circle. Then there was silence, and all heads turned to Randolph Dikkon for his judgment.

Chapter Three
Cricket and Critics

He of the long white beard combed it for a moment, intently eyeing the prisoner, and the latter, as though wearied of the cricket, now stood up and raised above his head his roped hands. He stretched, rising on tiptoe, and the ropes that bound his hands together creaked mightily. At that, six-guns appeared swiftly from beneath six coats, but the ropes held, and the prisoner's hands fell before him once more.

"I guess I'd better be going," he said.

Oliver Dikkon met him and caught his arm. "You sit down where you were," he said sternly.

The big man looked down on the other without malice and, nodding his head cheerfully, he answered: "All right, if that's what you want."

He sat down. He searched with sudden care for the cricket, found it, and replaced it on the bear rug. Then he settled back to a more earnest contemplation of its peculiarities. At last Randolph Dikkon spoke.

"We've got our man at last," he said, "and John says that he's admitted what we all know that he's done. I dunno what more we could ask for, and I guess that we've got trees high enough to do what we want of them. Eustace, you'd better take charge of him, and the quicker you get the thing over with the better for him . . . and for us."

Eustace rose accordingly, with a slight hardening, if that were possible, of his features and approached the prisoner.

"Stand up, Barney Quince!" he commanded.

The prisoner rose, and he smiled his beautiful smile at the little, frost-bitten Eustace.

At this, Oliver Dikkon started out of his chair and crossed to the pair. He tapped his elder cousin, Eustace, on the shoulder.

"Hold on a minute, Eustace," he said.

"You always was fond of talking, Oliver," said the older man. "But I dunno that talk will serve us now. There's a hanging to be got done with, Oliver."

"I was just thinking . . . you're a man who's always handled dogs a good deal, Eustace."

"And there's only one way to deal with a mad dog," said Eustace readily enough.

There was a deep-throated murmur of assent, and Oliver nodded agreement. "Certainly, you're right. But tell me, Eustace, when a puppy comes into your house and tears up a hat or a pair of riding boots, what do you do to it?"

"Thrash it, of course, and teach it better sense," said Eustace. "Stand out of my way, Oliver!" He said the last with a tone of anger, for Oliver Dikkon had interposed between him and the prisoner.

"I still have something to say," replied Oliver, "and I guess it's the rule with us that everybody has a chance to talk out what's in his head until Uncle Randolph overrules him. Is that right, sir?"

He of the white beard nodded gravely. "Go on and talk, lad," he said. "I guess that nobody could improve on what you sometimes got to say! What's bothering you now?"

"I say," declared Oliver, "that there's no more difference between a grown dog and a puppy than there is between the Barney Quince that killed our men and the Barney Quince that's here in front of us now."

This speech made a sensation, and hard-bitten Eustace said with a sneer: "You kind of like this giant, Oliver. You kind of take to him, it seems to me."

To this Oliver said sadly: "I hope I've proved myself as

good a Dikkon as you have, Eustace, though you're a good deal older than I am, and I suppose that you're wiser in most things. But I want to point out that nobody has lost much more than I have through this man. It was he that came down and burned my whole wheat crop and barn on my river farm, as anyone can remember. And my two nephews that were raised about as much in my house as in their own . . . I mean poor Charlie and Peter . . . they both were killed by this man. I mean to say that I've got reasons both of hard cash and blood to hate him, and I think that I hate him as much as most of you do. But I got a couple of things to point out to you.''

There was a restless turning of heads to Randolph Dikkon but, since the old man said nothing at once, Martin Glanvil spoke up in his deep and growling voice: "Facts is facts, and blood is blood. Unless they can be swallowed, this here man has got to die, Oliver.''

"Wait a minute," broke in Randolph Dikkon. "We've got to hear everything that Oliver has to say, if he keeps us here all night. Go on, Oliver!''

"Thanks," said Oliver. "Then I'll talk up and say what I've got to say. I want to remind you of the time when Bud and Luke, Sam Dikkon's two boys, started out and swore that they'd never leave the trail until they'd found Quince. They found him, as you might remember. It was winter. They got to a shack, and there they found the signs of Quince. They stayed there until the dark came down, and they lay quiet, ready to kill him when he opened the door.

"Well, he did open the door at last, and they turned loose at him. He fell down in the snow with a bullet through his left leg and, lying there, he shot them both. They surrendered to him wounded like he was, and they. . . .''

"By heaven," cried Eustace, "I'm not gonna listen to this!''

"Steady! Steady!" said little Henry Dikkon. "We've got to take the bitter with the sweet.''

"Then," went on Oliver, "he crawled in and took their

guns. Bud was drilled right through the body, and Luke was shot through the shoulder so bad that his arm ain't any good today. And Quince stayed there in the cabin with his game leg and helped to tie up their wounds. For two months he kept them, and then he turned them loose, safe and sound, and let them ride down to the valley again. And Bud and Luke to this day . . . they never will say a word against him. Is that all a fact, or do I make it up?''

A gloomy silence answered this statement and appeal.

Finally the speaker went on: ''Now, here we got Barney Quince. Did we go hunting for him? We did not! Did we get him by a fair fight? We did not! Did we buy him from his enemies even? We did not! But he walked in and gave himself up, you might say, because he'd been hurt worse than through the body or the leg. He's gone in the brain, and there he is for any of you to see that he's got an empty brain. Now, men, I say that the killing of a man like that is worse than the murder of a baby, and I'll work and fight against it as long as I've got a thought in my head and a drop of blood in my body.''

''You think,'' said Eustace bitterly, ''that, because you stand in with him now, he'll stand in with you later on when he's better!''

''How can he get better, once his wits have left him?'' asked Oliver. ''Look at him, will you? Studying a cricket while we try him for his life.''

''Maybe he's playing 'possum,'' suggested Glanvil sternly.

''Did that bring him down into the middle of our town?'' asked Oliver Dikkon.

''Speak up, Uncle Randolph,'' urged Eustace in the greatest excitement, ''and tell 'em that they're gonna bring down blood on their heads if they let this gent live.''

But Randolph Dikkon said not a word. Finally Henry broke in: ''I dunno how it is, but I got to agree with Oliver. That ain't a man there. It used to be Barney Quince. It's the size and the shape of Barney Quince still, but it's just an empty shell, it seems to me. There's nothing inside of it because a man with his wits gone is like a nut with the meat out of it. Killing Barney, here, you ain't killing the man that done the shooting of so many of our clan. It's like killing a stranger that never lifted a hand in his life to hurt nobody."

This speech made two on the side of the prisoner, and all faces became grave.

John Dikkon burst out: "I say that I hate the face and the name of him, and no harm can be done by putting him out of the way. Let it be done legally, if you want. But let it be done. Bring him up for trial then."

"Bring him for trial before Judge Postlethwaite," said Henry Dikkon, "and he'll send him to a home for the feeble-minded before the trial's a day old. Ask your own good sense, John, and you'll see that that's true."

The lawyer was silenced, though he shook his head in a sullen denial that had no meaning.

"Uncle Randolph, will you give us a judgment, here?"

The old man sighed.

"There's no good going to come of it," he said, "but, when two and two is put together, you got to say that it adds up four, and the two and two that you name here, it looks to me that it adds up to what Oliver says. This man is no more than a baby. The Dikkons never have loved the Quinces, but we never have been baby-killers. I guess that's about the end of things. Call Louise, Oliver, and ask her to get me a cup of coffee. I kind of have a need for it before I go home in the cold."

Oliver went gladly to obey the order but, before he reached the door, Eustace whirled upon the others and raised a thin hand above his head. It was quivering with his wrath.

"I hear you talk, you gents," he said. "I hear you talk, and it's all very fine what you got to say. You talk about babies and such. But I talk about Barney Quince, and I tell you that you'll never again have the chance that you've got now. Here he is that's done all of the murders and, if you let him go, you'll never have the like chance again. God forgive you all if you set him free to start on the trail again. More of us'll be hunted down. For the fifteen that he's killed already, a hundred is apt to drop before the finish. Besides, he'll have the time and the chance to leave a son behind him to carry on for the name of Quince where he left off. I've got no part in this decision. I say that you're a parcel of fools. I'm going home, and I'll be damned if ever I come to another council of the Dikkons. Get another to take my place!''

Chapter Four
A Devoted Servitor

The head of Barney Quince healed in due time and never for an instant did it make him an invalid. He was constantly about the house of Oliver Dikkon, sometimes wandering into the fields and sometimes climbing about the great lofts of the barn, where he seemed to take a peculiar pleasure in getting as far aloft as possible. Then, sitting on a great cross-beam or dizzily poised on the derrick rod which projected above the door of the mow, he would fall into brooding. Time seemed to him of no more moment than it is to a roosting owl. At night he slept in the hay, and often on the coldest nights he stretched himself on a mat in the kitchen in front of the stove. His long life in the wilderness had made the softness of a bed apparently distasteful to him.

He was not altogether simple, even though it seemed impossible for him to understand most of the words which were spoken to him. For instance, he allowed no tear to appear in his clothes without sitting down at once to mend it with a scrupulous fineness of handiwork which no woman could have surpassed. His skill at this suggested to Louise Dikkon other means of employing him, so that he might be useful to the family which supported him now and also to himself. The doctor of the village of Adare could only suggest that constant occupation would be better for the poor, deranged, stunned mind.

Barney Quince was at the disposal of Lou Dikkon because, from the first day, he looked upon her with a great attachment—not as a man to a woman but rather as a dog to a master. He would follow her about the house for hours. If she sat down to her sewing, he sat down cross-legged on the floor nearby and seemed perfectly contented. If she went for a walk, he ranged with her, wandering with his rapid step here and there, sometimes running to a distance but always circling back. Her father was alarmed at this constant attendance, but gradually everyone came to understand that Barney Quince was utterly harmless.

So Louise began to employ this useless, mighty engine. She tried him at first at the woodpile where the dried oak, hard as flint from the seasoning it had received, had to be sawed into convenient lengths and then split. With her own hands she put the heavy and cumbersome cross-cut in position and guided it for him. For the greater part of a day she worked at the lesson before he could learn what was wanted. Then he sawed through a segment readily enough and, as he grew warm with the work and rolled up his sleeves, she watched the sinewy muscles playing snake-like up and down his forearms. Then she understood why the warriors who were the pride of Adare had been helpless in the hands of this giant, and she felt a great awe, much as may be felt by a trainer who compels lions to do trifling tricks.

It was very hard to make progress with him. When he had sawed through a log, he would come into the house bearing a ponderous section in his hands and offer it to her with a smile of childish joy. She had to lead him back and replace the great saw at the proper point. It was a week before he could understand the whole business of wood-sawing, but after that he advanced into the huge pile of timber like a fire. When the sawing was done, she taught him to split the chunks to appropriate sizes, and then with much patience she instructed him in cording the wood in the shed. He seemed to feel no burden in these labors; and sometimes she would pause in her kitchen work, hearing out of the distance a great voice that swelled into a phrase or two of song. Only a little moment of music and then a long silence, as though the fumbling brain had picked up a happy thread only to lose it again almost at once.

After this start had been made with him, it was increasingly easy to teach him other tasks. She taught him to milk the string of cows and pour the milk into the pans in the creamery. How to churn, and how to fork down the hay for the teams so that their mangers were filled when they came in from work at the plow. She even attempted to teach him to work the plow, but in this she failed utterly, for he persisted in leaving the team standing in the field while he came back to the house to her. At any distance from her he was unhappy, bewildered, and through the day he had to come to her again and again and stand silently by, reading her face with an expression half intent and half wistful.

She became fascinated by her duties as schoolmistress and tried him at reading and writing, but here she had no success whatever. For though he might sit down and write off a whole sentence at dictation with a rapid and flowing hand, yet in the middle of a word the machine might stop and refuse to start again that day. In the meantime, however, he had become a profitable worker and Oliver Dikkon, estimating his value with a strict sense of honor, paid monthly wages into the hands of his daughter to be used for her protégé as she thought best.

She was seen walking down to the store, with the giant stepping softly behind her. He stood by, vaguely pleased, while she bought clothes for him or shoes. There was one heart-stopping moment when he paused by the rack where the rifles stood and, taking out one of the best, opened the chamber and reached with an automatic hand for a cartridge, fumbling blindly when he discovered that he was not girt with the long-familiar belt. However, he let her take the weapon from his hands, and she led him away, past the pale-faced clerks.

She talked to her father about this incident, and he considered it for a long time before he made the most unexpected answer.

"You've got to let a man work along the lines that he knows," said Oliver Dikkon. "A fine cowpuncher may be a fool at books, and a bookman may be a fool with cows. A good miner might die of dry rot being a clerk. So with Barney Quince that has lived by the gun for his whole life, pretty near ... maybe one thing that keeps him back is not having a rifle, say, and plenty of chance to use it!''

''And . . . ?'' she began.

''And if he should ever use it on a man . . . why the man would be dead, and we'd have to kill Barney. It's a hard chance to take. But I think that there's no danger in him now. There's no meanness, and there's no malice. I'm going to let you take him my best rifle tomorrow.''

She was full of fear, but she recognized sound reasoning behind this advice. That same day she placed the rifle in the grip of Barney Quince and put on him the cartridge belt. For two days he was helpless with joy, sitting with the gun in his lap, admiring its brightness, patting it like a living creature. The third day he was found cleaning it. The fourth day he disappeared!

Terror ran through the entire village of Adare. Swift messengers were sent to outlying workers in the fields. In dread and in silence they waited. But in the evening a giant walked from the shadows of the trees and strode across the fields carrying on his shoulders a deer which would have been well nigh a burden for a horse. He kicked open the kitchen door and laid it at the feet of Lou Dikkon. Then he stood by, panting with his vast labor, and laughing out of the joyous fullness of his heart. All Adare breathed once more.

After that, there was hardly a day when he did not slip off from his other duties and hunt in the fields, in the woods, over the hills. He brought back rabbits, squirrels whose heads had been clipped off as though with a shears, deer, partridges. The larder of Oliver Dikkon's place was crammed with fresh meat, and his neighbors came to bless the gun of Barney Quince. It was at this period also, as the spring turned warm, that he was put on the trail of the lame grizzly which for three seasons had devastated the valleys, choosing with a nice taste the best of the yearling colts, dining once upon each body and then departing to come again.

For a week Barney Quince was gone, and Eustace Dikkon vowed that he would never be seen any more. He was seen, however. With a great bearskin rolled on the back of a burro, he trudged home to the house of Oliver Dikkon and laid the massive spoils before his mistress.

From that moment the attitude of Adare toward Barney Quince altered perceptibly, for up to this time the villagers had looked upon him as a public menace, a danger postponed but inevitably sure to fall. Thereafter it was felt that his old identity had been lost forever, and that he had become a public benefactor. Moreover, they derived a rather sinister satisfaction from the knowledge of what he had been, and what he now was. When they saw him striding down the street behind his mistress, resolutely refusing to walk at her side, they could not help smiling, one to another, for this was as it should be with a Quince! He was better than dead. His old self had perished. He lived only to serve his enemies like another Samson with bonds not upon his body but on his brain.

Lou Dikkon was aware of the public attitude, but her own differed. She took great and greater care that he should not be made an open show. When small boys formed the habit of running after them, her father was sent to call on their parents. Gradually people came to know that Oliver Dikkon and his daughter respected this hulk which once had been so great a ship, and for the sake of Oliver Dikkon the smiles were ended.

So the bright heat of summer came to Adare, and with it came the usual thin drift of Easterners, arriving for a vacation among the mountains. Most important of these holiday-makers was that great and good man, Dr. Mansfeld, from New York. On the very first day of his arrival he passed on the street the smiling face and the blank eye of the giant, and he stopped short and turned to look after him. Of course, he had already heard the story. And that night he came to the house of Oliver Dikkon and asked to see this stricken man.

He found Lou Dikkon at the piano, drawing accompaniments out of its untuned strings, while she sang like a bird. Leaning on the piano, stood Barney Quince. He allowed his head to be examined with perfect indifference. Afterwards, when Lou went to bed, he went after her to lie in the hallway across her door. The doctor remained behind with Oliver Dikkon.

Chapter Five
Who Are You?

The doctor went straight to the point. It needed no special skill, he declared, to tell what was wrong with Barney Quince. It was the fall which had stunned him, of course, that had made him a half-wit or something little better. The reason he remained in that condition was simply that a segment of skull had been permanently depressed and bore down upon the brain. Now, there was one chance in ten that an operation would kill the patient. There were four chances in ten that the operation would do him no good. There were five chances in ten that he would be completely cured and made as intelligent a man as ever he had been before.

Oliver Dikkon listened, growing more and more tense, and his brown face lengthened with gravity. Finally he said: "Suppose you win with him, Doctor Mansfeld. Then what'll he be?"

"An intelligent, alert man once more."

"D'you know what kind of a man he was?"

"I've heard that he was a rough character, but his experiences recently, no doubt, will have tamed him. You have been kind to him, Mister Dikkon. That kindness can't be forgotten."

Oliver Dikkon mused: "When he got the blow on the head, it wiped his memory clean. Lift the bone and probably he'll go back to the time when he had the fall. Ain't that possible?"

"It is," agreed the doctor unhappily.

"Fifteen men have been killed by Barney Quince," said Dikkon. "They were all my kin. Ten of 'em lived in Adare.

35

I say that if you bring him back to his wits, so's he'll remember his own name, then he has to stand trial for fifteen killings, and the trial will be before a jury of Dikkons, and there ain't any doubt of what the verdict would be. You'd only be saving him to hang him, Doctor! If he didn't hang but got away, there's many a strong and brave man alive today that'll die under the guns of Barney Quince before he's ended with a bullet through his head.''

All of this the doctor considered, and he could see the strength in the argument. Yet he was pushed on by earnest devotion to his art. He argued: "Quince is already dead, and this poor creature who fills his body is neither man nor beast.''

"He's a man!'' insisted Dikkon. "He does a man's work, too, and he's worth his pay. I'd rather have him the way he is than any other two men on my ranch. What more do you ask for him? He's happy. He loves my daughter. She can make him do anything. She's teaching him a little more and more all the time. Maybe he'll wake up entire, one of these days, except that he won't know he's Barney Quince and born and raised to kill me and my family. Ain't there a chance . . . that he'll get pretty normal, I mean?''

"There is no more chance of that,'' said the doctor, "than there is that he'll walk to the moon. I leave this matter on your conscience, Mister Dikkon. If I were in your place, I should not like to have on my mind that I've stood between this man and his true self.'' With that, he left.

Two days later Dikkon came to the hotel where Mansfeld was putting the finishing touches to his preparations for the mountains.

"I've talked it over with my daughter,'' he said. "I didn't call in the older heads of my people because I knew beforehand what they'd say. I've talked it over with my daughter, and she's been driving me on to it. If you say the word, she'll bring Quince in to you whenever you wish.''

So that matter was arranged, and the doctor hurried on with his work, arranged for a room that would serve for the operation, found by keenest good luck a skilled assistant, and prepared his instruments.

Early the next morning, Lou Dikkon came to the hotel, and behind her walked Barney Quince. She stood in front of great Dr. Mansfeld and said to him, all pale and still of eye: "If ever Barney Quince kills another man, Doctor, what will you think about it?"

The doctor did not like this view of the matter. He said something about the necessity for serving the will of nature with the skill of science. But he was so ill at ease that he rushed on with the preparations, and soon Barney Quince was alone with the doctor, his assistant, and half a dozen strong fellows who were to help during the anesthetizing process.

That process had hardly begun before there was a violent disturbance in the operating room. Wild cries were heard. The door was split clean in two, from top to bottom, and Barney Quince rushed out, shaking off the last man to cling to him. Lou Dikkon blocked his escape and, taking his hand, she led him back into the operating room. At sight of it his nostrils flared, and a dull light glowed in his eyes. But at her direction he lay down again on the table, and he allowed her hands to tie on him the bonds which had driven him frantic before. Then she explained the process of anesthetizing as well as she could. It was plain that all was a cloud to his weak understanding, but he clung to her hand and fixed his great, doglike eyes upon her.

"It's all right, Lou?" he asked her.

"It's all right," she said.

She stood by with her hand resting upon his shoulder, and so stood while he lay without the slightest motions of resistance. She grew dizzy with the fumes of the ether. The doctor pronounced the state of unconsciousness complete, and she was allowed to leave the room. But as she reached the door, a shout and a sudden struggle called her back.

The giant had ripped across the cloths which tied his hands, and four men vainly were striving to keep him from sitting up. Lou hurried back, and in a few seconds the patient lay passively under her hand.

"It seems," said the doctor in deep bewilderment, "to be rather hypnosis than ether. You'll have to stay here, my dear young lady."

Stay there she did and closed her eyes to keep out the sight of what was being done. But she could not keep out the sound of hammer on chisel head, or the hideous dull noise of chisel on bone, or the sound of the saw, or the low voice of Dr. Mansfeld pointing out details to his assistant as he proceeded.

Once, indeed, she opened her eyes. There was a whirl of confusion, in the midst of which the doctor raged with terrible fluency and volume. Black mists rose before her eyes. But then she steadied herself and clutched her fingers into the quivering muscles of Barney's shoulder. After that, there was quiet again. She began to reel with weakness.

Still the work went on, and the long silence continued. Still she dared not look. Perhaps this doctor with his demonic skill was taking her out of the soul of poor Barney Quince with chisel and saw.

"Lou!" said a choked voice.

"Steady, steady!" she murmured.

The giant was still once more, and her heart leaped with a wildly selfish joy. He had spoken her name—her memory, then, had not been wiped out!

She felt there was something of devilish magic in this labor of Mansfeld's. But in the meantime, she was chained to her post, though her knees began to tremble. Then a hand touched her shoulder, and a voice said quietly: "Drink this, Miss Dikkon!"

She looked up into the face of the doctor. His bristling, wax-tipped mustache, his glittering eyes, and his pointed beard made her feel that she was staring at some devil incarnate. She drank what he held at her lips—something pungent and stinging.

"Courage!" he said. "Without you, we can do nothing! Courage and strength, my dear child!"

He patted her shoulder, but she knew that there was no kindness in the touch. It was totally perfunctory. She happened to be, for him, a necessary instrument at this moment, and therefore she was worth conciliation—until the work had ended. But the drink gave her fresh strength.

Another long, dreary interval passed. A buzzing came in her ears and, through the buzzing, a voice boomed distantly: "She's going to faint, I think."

"Let her faint . . . the job's finished!"

That was the voice of Dr. Mansfeld, like the booming of a cannon. Afterwards, faint she did and felt arms receive her. She shook off the weakness instantly as she heard a groan from the man on the table. That was the shock that cleared her brain again and enabled her to stand to her task. Someone was explaining something to her

Ah, yes! The operation was finished.. It was successful! Now, if she would walk beside the stretcher as they carried the patient only into the very next room . . . ? She walked beside it with fumbling steps. Fresh, untainted air blew about her from the open windows, and then she was sitting beside the bed of the patient.

Up and down the room walked Dr. Mansfeld. He was speaking. She heard only snatches, as he talked about difficulties—uncertainties—pressure on the brain—the brain itself—the mystery of thought. She hardly knew what all these long combinations of words meant, but she knew that she was ordered to sit quietly there. She was willing to do that, for the face of the sleeper wore, in flashes, the same beautiful smile with which she was so familiar. When he awakened, surely he would be the same. He stirred.

"He's going to waken," snapped the incisive voice of the doctor. "Now, my girl . . . you're fond of this fellow. Then lean over him. Imagine you're facing a camera. Look pleasant, please, and. . . ."

The eyes of Barney Quince opened. They were no longer blank but filled with a wildly delirious light. "Steady, Jerry . . . steady, you old fool." And then the voice rose to a great shout. Barney Quince sat up in bed. "Hello, hello!" he murmured. "That was a crash and . . . who are you?" he asked and looked straight into the face of Lou Dikkon.

Chapter Six
Successful Operations

Somehow she was out of the room and feeling her way blindly down the stairs. At the bottom brilliant sunshine blazed before her. She put her hand to her face and found it wet.

"I mustn't cry," she said aloud, and feebly. "I've got to be steady, steady!"

So she took a firm hold on herself, and made her step light as she reached the street. A shadow came up beside her and took her arm.

"What happened?" asked her father.

She clung to him weakly. "Get me home . . . I'll try to talk there," she said.

So they hurried together, but it seemed that the little village street had been stretched out to weary, stumbling miles before the familiar door of the house opened to them. She lay on the parlor couch, her eyes closed and her father holding her hand.

He was saying very gently: "It was too bad. I didn't want the chance to be taken. But he said it was only one in ten, you know. And, after all . . . poor fellow! What was there in life for him, Lou? I'm sorry too, though. It chokes me actually. There, there, honey. You cry. It'll do you good."

She shook her head. "It isn't what you think," she managed to say. "He's alive, but he's worse than dead to all of us. He's forgotten me. He's the old Barney Quince!"

In the hospital, the doctor ordered quiet and, when he heard that sharp incisive voice of the patient, he leaned above him and said in a tone of command: "Quince, you're all right now.

You've had a bad accident. You'll have to lie still. In two weeks, perhaps, you'll be able to leave. Perhaps a month. Perhaps ten days. You seem to have the strength. But now, you'll have to lie still. Do you understand?''

Barney Quince looked at him from thoughtful eyes and said nothing at all. But he obeyed the orders with the strictest patience, and for many and many a day he lay still and studied the ceiling and spoke not at all, except to say good morning and good evening.

Then the doctor came back. He had been away on a brief excursion, and he visited his patient before the next mountain trip was undertaken. He came in cheerfully and found himself looking down into a pair of stern and quiet eyes. It seemed to the doctor that never before had he looked at a face so heroically formed for strength or so beautiful in feature.

"Well, Quince," he said, "how are you?"

"Able to ride, thank you," said Barney Quince.

"As soon as this?"

"I'm able to ride," repeated the patient.

"Perhaps in a short time but not yet. Has the time gone slowly with you?"

"No," replied the other, "because I've lain here and had a chance to think things out . . . only there's a lot that I can't piece together."

"Have you asked any questions?"

"No."

"None?" exclaimed the doctor in astonishment.

"People always tell you what's really worth hearing and good for you. And the other sort . . . why, it ain't worth asking for, is it?"

The doctor smiled a little at this rather profound philosophy. Then he sat down and lighted a cigar.

"What do you last remember . . . before you came to?" he asked of the patient.

"I remember my horse sliding down a bank and losing his balance when the pebbles began to slip under him. Then I crashed. It was like being hit hard on the point of the chin. That was all. After that, I woke up here.''

The doctor nodded. ''Nothing in between?

''No.''

''Not a thing, then?''

''No, it's a blank.''

''Shall I fill in the blank for you?''

''If you want to.''

The doctor began to drum the tips of his fingers against the arm of his chair, always regarding the sick man with an intent gaze. ''You'd better find it out for yourself,'' he said then. ''It may be a lot better that way. Do you know where you are now?''

''I got an idea.''

''What is it?''

''It's a thing that I don't like to talk about.''

''Ah?''

''Because I figure that I'm in Adare.''

''It's true.''

''And I'd rather be in any other place.''

The doctor nodded. ''I've heard a little bit about the trouble between you and these townsmen,'' he admitted. ''But now I want to give you a little advice that isn't exactly medical. You can't leave this place, Quince. They've put guards under your window and at your door. You have no weapons. The thing for you to do is to stand your trial like a law-abiding citizen. Face justice, Quince. It's always the best way. Forget your old life and prepare yourself for a new one.''

Barney Quince smiled, but his only answer was to ask quietly: ''Where would I be tried?''

''Here in Adare, of course.''

''The judge would be a Dikkon,'' he said, ''and all the jury would be their men.''

Dr. Mansfeld rubbed his chin and found no more to say. He received the thanks of Barney Quince, and presently he squared his shoulders in the outer day and turned his thoughts

43

to the upper mountains. He had done his work, and he had done it well. As for the consequences, after all he could not pretend to be both a doctor and the body of the law.

So Barney Quince was left alone and, now that he knew the situation he was in, he adapted himself to it as swiftly as he could. The doctor had ordered another fortnight of absolute rest for his patient, and the men of Adare were not prepared to arrest their enemy until the medical man had pronounced him fit to go to jail. This much they would make sure of, lest afterward the law should be brought down upon their own heads. In the meantime they kept their guard in place, changing it at regular intervals.

It was a costly business to tie up so much man power, but the expense of it and the trouble were small things to them. The important point was that Quince lay in their power, and therefore they made the net strong and waited with unwavering patience for the appointed day.

Barney Quince was laboring to bring back the strength which he had lost by lying so long prone. It was no easy task, for a dozen times by day and a dozen times by night the door of his room would be softly opened and someone would look in upon him silently, and silently the head would be withdrawn after making sure that all was well. He could not even be sure of the intervals between these espials. Sometimes he might have two hours free from disturbance. Sometimes not two minutes elapsed between the spying glances that were turned upon him.

To circumvent this crafty observance, he used the utmost patience. Lying in his bed, he went regularly through small movements which would exercise his muscles—such as arching his body on head and heels, or thrusting himself up from his spread arms, or lifting both legs and keeping them raised until the great thigh muscles shuddered with effort. All of these things he could do with movements which were utterly noiseless and which needed hardly the slightest disturbance of the covers of his bed. The result of these patient exercises was that the discarded mantle of his strength gradually returned to him, his chest arched, and power tingled down his arms to the tips of his fingers.

Yet, with the strength regained, it was no easy matter to use it for his escape. He lay on his side at the edge of his bed and scanned the ceiling and the wall. They were of smooth, newly made plaster and could not be broken without noise. Then he stole to the window at midnight and looked down to the street. It was a sheer descent of twenty feet, much too far to be jumped, and just opposite he saw two riflemen seated, waiting patiently, should he attempt to climb down, both wide awake even at this hour.

The window and the ceiling and the walls were hopeless as outlets, and beyond the door waited the second guard. There remained the floor. It was of tough strips of pine, held down with new nails, and covered, in part, with a rag rug. Through that floor, nevertheless, he knew that he must go, and constantly it was in his thoughts. He had one tool: a pocket knife which they had disdained to deprive him of because the longest blade was well under two inches in length. However, with that tool he had finally determined to attack his problem.

To be sure, the blades were short, but they were wide and strong and made of the very finest steel, with chisel edges. He fell to work. Lying on his side, the cot was so very low that he could reach the floor with either hand. He turned back the rag rug and began. If three of the sections of the boards could be cut through and lifted out, then there would remain beneath him the lath and plaster work of the ceiling below. But the laths could be cut through quickly enough, he could be sure.

He started, conscious that there were two great dangers to its consummation. One was the fear that the spies at the door might look in upon him and find him at his labor. The second was the terror lest the rag rug should be stripped off the floor and taken out to be beaten. On Saturdays that work was usually done. This was Tuesday on which he was commencing his work, and he must trust that the daily sweeping would be done without disturbing the rug too much. As for the constant spyings, he trained himself to baffle the spies. He never worked except during daylight, and then with one eye he constantly regarded the knob of the door. It was kept so well oiled that it could be turned without the slightest sound, but it could not be turned without the motion becoming visible. Watching that, the instant there was the slightest disturbance the rag rug was jerked back into place, and the prisoner-patient was discovered lying on his face on the cot.

This required that his nerves should be drawn to the breaking point at all hours of the day, but it was a price which he had to pay, and he paid it willingly. As for the cuts he made in the boards, the long strips of the tough wood that he whittled away were tucked into the mattress on which he lay, for he had made an opening in a seam for that very purpose. He made the cuts very wide, which facilitated rapid cutting, but the instant the rug was moved he would be discovered. It was a peril which he had to accept.

He did the cutting, first, at the point which he had chosen farthest down from the head of the bed. It required until Wednesday night to complete that work. Then he attacked the upper cut and went through it in a single day of hardly interrupted labor. And still he had all Friday before him—his escape he planned for Friday night.

As he tucked the last shaving into the mattress and with a smile patted down the hard little lump of wood which had been formed there under the seam, the door opened with its usual softness. Eustace Dikkon entered and came to the bedside, and with him was a spectacled gentleman. The latter set out stethoscope, thermometer, and the rubber tubing of the instrument for taking blood pressure. Then he began his examination and went over every inch of the leonine body of the sick man. Eustace Dikkon stood by with no expression in his rock-like face.

"Temperature normal," said the doctor. "Pulse normal and strong. Heart excellent. Blood pressure normal. Muscular condition excellent. In fact, I've never heard of a man in bed so long whose muscles retained their temper so well. I should say, Mister Dikkon, that this man is perfectly sound in every way . . . infinitely above the average. He's in a super-normal state of health.''

Eustace Dikkon let his eyes rest for a single instant on the face of the captive and never was malice and determined hatred more plainly visible. That single, glowing glance and then he withdrew from the room.

Young Barney Quince lay rigidly in the bed. Somewhere out of the distance a clock was striking. He never had heard it before, but now all his faculties were roused by excitement to a super-sensibility, and he tolled off the faint pulse of the sound. It was ten o'clock and, as fast as Eustace Dikkon could prepare adequate quarters in the jail, Barney Quince would be brought there to wait for his death.

Chapter Seven
Beyond the Wall

A stir began in the hotel—a passing of many feet to and fro, the sound of subdued voices in the halls, and the sharp creaking of the stairs under the weight of people who hastened up and down. Barney Quince slipped softly from his bed, from the closet took shirt and trousers, and stepped into them. As for shoes, he was better off without them for his purposes. As he turned from the closet, the door of the hall yawned open swiftly and silently, and a great shaft of light beat into the room. His first impulse was to leap straight at the spy; but softly the door was shut again. He heard no sound of hurrying feet or any exclamation.

Might it not be that, glancing at the ruffled clothes of the bed, the watcher had told himself that Barney Quince was still there? A thousand times they had looked in, in this fashion, and a thousand times all had been well. However, there must be no such sudden interruption as this in the moments that followed.

He picked up the one chair, stole close to the wall—where there was far less chance that a floor board would creak under foot—and then to the door. With the greatest care he braced the back of the chair under the doorknob. Returning to the side of the bed, he threw back the rag rug. There was a dim light faintly filling the room, from the great gasoline lamp which burned until midnight over the entrance to Whitney's Stables across the street. By that light, as he raised the pine board through which he had cut, he could examine the work which remained under his hand. The lathing was wide but the

48

strips were thin, as if made to order for his purpose.

All the great power of his wrist went into his work as, making the notches wide, he labored around the edge of the gap in the floor. There were a hundred grittings of the knife against the grains of the plaster. Twice the blade squeaked in the wood, but the disturbances continued throughout the hotel and the noises he made were apparently confused with what was heard elsewhere.

Once or twice he paused to listen and, in those pauses, he was aware of subdued murmurs in the hall outside his room, murmurs of many men gathering there. It was certain that Eustace Dikkon was making surety doubly sure by marshaling a little army to conduct the prisoner to the jail. Then came a sharp crunch of wood against wood. The door had been thrust inward, but the chair stuck at once and yielded, screechingly, only a bit.

"What the devil is this?" exclaimed a roaring voice. "What deviltry is up here? Some of you boys put your shoulders against that door!"

Barney Quince was in a whirl of rapid action. The upper layer of the laths he had cut through. What remained below, beside the tough plaster, he could not guess. He swept the spread from his cot and wrapped it around his bare feet. Then he leaped into the air to the full of his power and brought down his two hundred pounds and the drive of his stamping legs in the center of the hole.

There was a crash in answer and a great sagging beneath him. At the same moment the door was struck by the weight of several strong men, yielded, then jerked open, the chair skidding before it. Half a dozen of the posse men spilled headlong into the room. Again Barney Quince leaped, and this time he drove straight through the lathing and the plaster work beneath him. Down he dropped as through a trapdoor. The rough edges of the lathing rasped at his clothes, ripped his body, but he fell headlong on the floor of the room beneath.

It was an unoccupied bedroom, as he saw when he sprang

to his feet and shook the dust from his face. Above him, pandemonium was breaking loose. Feet were thundering on the stairs, voices shouting. He leaped to the door. It was locked! Glancing upwards, he saw an arm ending in a revolver reach down.

It was like the flash of a spur in the eye of a frightened horse. Sideways Quince sprang at the door, and it split before him as though it were thinnest cardboard. Into the hallway he stumbled and lurched straight into the arms of two men who had turned onto the landing of the stairs at full speed.

They clung to him valiantly, but his impetus carried all three over the brink of the stairs and brought them whirling and crashing down. In a way it was as though Barney Quince were the core of a rolling ball. The impacts which he might have received were muffled by the bodies of those who clung to him and, as that spinning mass of humanity crashed against a lower, angling wall and lay still, Barney Quince rose from it to his feet. The other two remained motionless.

Something glimmered on the landing. He scooped it up, and now he stood armed with a loaded Colt. Half the barrier between him and freedom was already crossed. He was in a place of utmost peril, however. From the stairs above him a flood of armed men was descending, swerving around the landing places, thundering on the steps. Just below him the narrow lobby of the hotel was alive with men who had rushed in from the street. There was no escape by turning and striving to shoot his way through the numbers above him, but in the confusion beneath there was some hope.

The central light which hung from the lobby ceiling was quivering back and forth in a slow arc, so greatly had the old building been shaken by this turmoil. One shot from his Colt shattered it to bits, and a shower of burning oil flamed wildly down over the heads of those beneath. Yells of terror and pain went shrieking up. To either side the men of the clan split apart and, through the narrow channel between them, Barney Quince fled on racing, naked feet.

Straight in his face, and from either side, half a dozen guns belched fire at him, but those shots were aimed by guess and from quivering hands, and the target was running like a stricken deer. He leaped through the doorway, swerved, but the speed of his going made him lurch over the side of the front verandah. He landed in the soft, pulpy dust and so darted around the corner of the hotel.

Before him rose a tall board fence, a wall of blackness. A bullet jerked past his ear with a rising whine. With a bound and a throwing of his body to the side, Barney Quince rolled over the top of that fence and dropped into one instant's freedom from peril in the dark beyond.

Chapter Eight
Freedom

No, hardly a single instant of safety was his. Around the front of the hotel the pursuit was spilling and, though these clansmen had been unsteadied hitherto by the surprises with which they had been confronted, he knew that thereafter their aim would be almost as deadly as by day. Also he heard the back door of the hotel crash wide and the heavy impact of many of the pursuing men who leaped clear of the rear stoop and landed on the ground beyond. A brief instant of confusion covered the eyes of Barney Quince as with a veil. Then his head cleared, and he ran onwards.

He could run fast and far, but just beyond the village lay rough ground that would cut his feet to ribbons. Besides, what is the speed of a man on foot compared with the speed of a running horse? And horsemen would begin to rush out from the town of Adare to find him. They were mounting now in the street; the thunder of hoofbeats was beginning and the yelling of the riders!

He went straight on, crossing the vegetable garden in which his feet drove ankle-deep through the soft sod. Swinging in a high vault over the fence beyond, he found himself in a little corral. Half a dozen horses leaped and rushed to the farther side of the enclosure.

Out of the distance behind him yelled a voice: "He's at the horses! Chuck! Toby! Come on, boys! Don't give him time to saddle!"

Time to saddle? No, there was not a second to be spared for that but, crouching in the shadow of the fence, like a panther in a cattle yard, Barney Quince eyed that frightened knot of horseflesh. He saw one arched crest that lifted above the others, and he knew that whether he lived or died it must be upon the back of that horse.

There was no time for a hesitating, gentle approach, no time for a soothing word. He had to accost that group of horses like a charging beast. If he reached his target with his spring, then a ghost of hope could rise in him once more. If he missed, he was a dead man, and he knew it well.

So he leaped from the fence shadow and darted forward. They split before him, rearing and squealing in their haste, but past a snaky head that snapped savagely at him he swerved and saw his chosen horse plunging to get through the mass and escape. He aimed for the mane with his hands and missed it but, as he leaped, his legs coiled around the shuddering loins of the horse, and a squeal of terror answered him.

He was nearly torn from his place by the lunge of the great animal. A smaller gelding went down before the big mare. Barney Quince was in the seat now, and one hand was twisted deeply in the flying mane as the horse hurled herself into the air.

"He's got a horse! By heaven, he's got Christie!" shouted someone from the fence top.

A gun flashed, and a bullet sang. Aye, they shot close to the mark by day or by night, the clan of Dikkon, but the great glimmering bay whirled Barney Quince around the corral like a flying comet. She crashed through the scattering herd again, and he was nearly torn from his place as she plunged clear, bucking madly still. No stirrup or girth or pommel to cling to, no spurs to lock in the cinches, no cantle to keep him in place, still he clung like a bit of her own flesh, and she flashed around the circle again.

It was a maelstrom of wheeling, squealing horses. A thick cloud of dust darkened the air like a fog. Guns flashed through the mist, and there was the groan and fall of a stricken horse. What purpose, however, in milling here, while the clan gathered around the corral? Yet how to break free? Certainly no kind hand would set the gate ajar for him!

He transferred his gun to the hand which was tangled in the mane. Then he reached back with his free fingers and sank them in the soft flesh of his mount's flank. He closed his hand and turned it. The result was a veritable scream of agony from the tortured mare, and she flung straight away at the fence. It was built high to hold wild creatures from the plains and none wilder than she had ever stood within it, yet she soared toward it like a bird. Her heels cracked in a sharp tattoo on the upper bar, and then she was over and rushing faster than the wind across the open ground beyond.

Bucking could not dislodge this torturing devil that clung to her. Then she would daze and bewilder him with the sheer speed of her flight. Yes, like an arrow she drove through the darkness. A black cloud rolled before them—trees and no reins to turn the flying mare. Clinging close, Quince leaned far over and prayed for luck. Boughs reached him like tearing hands, branches scourged his face like the lashes of whips, but then they were through.

Before them water flashed, but the mare rose nobly at it. A broad, pale face, it gleamed below them—then she was across with a shock on the farther bank that nearly tore Barney Quince from his place. Scrambling cat-like up the slope, she broke through the farther screen of trees—and before them rolled the hills and the sacred heads of the mountains high against the stars.

Still she flew, and Quince laughed with savage joy as he felt her speed. Let them try to follow, no matter how light their weights, how good their saddles, how keen their horsemanship. For where is there a saddle so good as fear? Where is there a spur so sharp as utter terror?

Then he began to soothe her with a gentle voice, his hand on her neck and passing gently back over the flank which he had torn at with his grip of iron. She heeded nothing. She was sleek, dripping, slippery from sweat; foam flew whitely back from her mouth, open as though a cruel curb were tearing at it.

They rocked over the hilltops and pitched wildly down into the hollows. Not till the first long slope of the upper mountains rose before her did the mare's gallop slacken and fall first to a staggering canter, then to a trot. She was beaten at last, but only after such a burst as those hard-riding men of Adare never could match with their best and bravest. From a wall of the gulch up which they were passing, Quince tore a long arm of trailing vine. From this he made a rope which he knotted about the mare's neck and then slipped to the ground.

She came to a dead halt, head down, ears falling loosely forward, legs braced. He felt her heart. It thundered with a rapid hammering against his hand, jarring his whole arm and body. A little more and she was dead!

He had to beat her down to the edge of the boiling creek. Once there, she stood shuddering, sagging at the knees, untempted by the cold water that foamed under her very muzzle. He began to wash her down, whistling a little, to occupy her attention while he swished cold water over her legs, over her neck, and then gradually rubbed down her body. For a long and aching time he labored over her, until at last she gathered her legs under her and reached for the water.

He allowed her only a swallow then dragged her tired head away and walked her up the cañon floor. Every few minutes he paused and rubbed her vigorously again. Then he passed on, tugging her after him. There was not strength enough in the vine rope. He had to drag her by the mane and sting her flank with his open hand to keep her in motion. It seemed that she never would come back to herself.

The gray of the dawn began as they climbed wearily out of the cañon and reached an upper tableland which made one mighty shoulder of old Mount Chisholm. There he paused, regarding the mare anxiously as the light grew. She was a red bay, long necked, deep of barrel, with, it seemed, Herculean quarters fit to bear the burden of the world. She seemed to have forgotten already, in her great and generous heart, the terror which she had felt for him. When he stood close, she laid her head against his breast and sighed like a weary child.

It seemed to Barney Quince, as he stroked her wet neck, that all the adventure of his stay in Adare—that strange and cloudy stretch of months of which he had no memory—and the fall in the mountains and the labor of his escape with all its perils had been preordained merely to bring into his hands this peerless creature. He tore up some bunch grass and offered it to her. Twice she sniffed it and turned her head away. He ripped up a bit more choice, dew moistened. This time she nibbled at it with feeble interest, and her ears raised and stiffened a little. Barney Quince stood back from her and laughed aloud. For he knew that that long battle for her life was ended, fought and won!

From the next runlet he let her drink but not her fill. Instead, he pulled her head away and went on slowly. In the back of his brain there was a great weariness, but he kept it out of his consciousness. All that he could be aware of was freedom, sweeter than wine to his taste.

He kept steadily on but, when he came to a tempting bit of pasture, he paused a little and let the mare graze, which she began to do greedily. She was coming back to normal rapidly. Her back no longer was partly arched, her belly no longer tucked up and gaunt and, though she stumbled now and then, when he had rubbed her down with twists of grass as the sun rose, nearly her whole strength seemed to have come back to her.

He turned now, high on the shoulder of Chisholm, and looked far down into the valley of Adare. He could not see the town because it was blanketed with blue morning mist, but the church steeple rose like a narrow blade of light. Barney Quince stood in the flaring face of the sun, and he laughed again.

Chapter Nine
Christie and Her Master

There were five shots remaining in the revolver of Barney Quince. With those five shots he killed a partridge and a rabbit the first day. The second day two more rabbits had to go to fill his hungry maw. On the third day he ate nothing at all but stalked ceaselessly to find bigger game. On the fourth day he slipped like a snake through a thicket and put a bullet into the heart of a deer just as it gathered its legs to leap.

For a week he lived on that meat and nothing else, and he lavished his time on Christie. It had taken her several days to recover entirely from the terrible strain of that flight from Adare, but now her full strength was back. She had forgotten the agony of her fear with which that ride began. She remembered instead the care and the kindness and the deep, soothing voice of the man in the time of her exhaustion. For let no one think that a horse cannot respond soul to soul, the animal to the man, both linked together by one common element of the divine. Christie had found her master, and she knew it with a profound certainty.

It was easy to teach her. She would follow Quince uncalled by the end of the second day; by the end of a week she would stand where he left her, grazing only in a small circle. At the pressure of his hand on her neck and the sound of a certain whisper, she would lower her sixteen-three of might and muscle to the earth and lie still, head stretched forth from the ground.

He trained her for mountain work. Indeed, mountain bred, it was not difficult for her to walk on a narrow ledge, or slide

57

down difficult slants, or pick her way among the sharp-toothed rocks. But though she improved greatly under his tutelage, still he knew that with that length of limb, that mighty bulk, she would never be a true mountaineer. She lacked that deer-like activity which is essential. The quick ups and downs broke her. Her wind left her in the labor of handling her own weight. No, she was meant not for dodging in and out along the coast, fighting the tidal roughs, clipping up narrow rivers and bays, skimming through shallows, turning in her own length, tacking like a restless midge. Instead she was meant for the open, like a great square-rigged clipper cleaving a way from China to the Thames. When once her swinging stride was driving her without effort, regardless of two hundred pounds on her back, running at half her power she could leave gasping and heart-broken behind her the very same cat-like mustangs which would catch her in no time among the hills.

These things Barney Quince pondered darkly. Those mountains were to him as home or home grounds are to most men. They were to him walls of safety, and the narrow and twisting ravines, and every cave, and every pothole, and the condition of every run in dry weather and wet, and all states of the passes according to the seasons, and all the upper trails, iced or piled with snow, were printed legibly in his memory. As it were, he turned the pages of a book and read at will. Should he abandon this, it was much indeed that he gave up.

He knew the valleys also, and the wide deserts and the rough, inhospitable plains into which they merged, chopped with sharp-edged draws, broken now and again by the high, ragged head of a mesa. But traveling there was different. He knew the water holes, and he knew many of the people, but the region was not so thickly dotted with his friends as were the mountains, where a few dollars spent with wise caution here and there ensured him of safe harborage and true friendship. On those perilous plains below, his enemies could hunt him glass in hand and dull beyond imagining would be the eyes that failed to recognize the looming outline of Christie with such a rider on her back!

There would be need of all her speed, down there, he had no doubt. They would bring out their Thoroughbreds, their flashiest speedsters to catch him. They would send afar off to experienced manhunters and mount them with the best and send them out to run him in relays.

Lying on the edge of a tableland that jutted out like the prow of a ship on the ridge between Lorimer Mountain and the Little Standup, he studied the lowlands for a hundred miles beneath him. Then he sat up and set his teeth. He was going down and let the Dikkon clan beware of his coming.

He started straight back for Adare, reached a thicket a few miles from it an hour before sunrise, and camped there for the day. Then he went on again when the night had gathered. It was the first time that he had come to pillage in the town itself. He had struck here and there on the outskirts. He had plundered outlying ranch houses of size. But he had not made his mark in the center of the town itself. The danger had seemed too great.

However, on this night he walked on into the village, with Christie left in a clump of poplars on the verge of the place. He looked about him with a calm eye of possession. To his distorted reason, all that he saw was as good as his. For, surely, it was true that the clan of the Quinces once had been stronger in numbers, richer in horses and land, than ever were the Dikkons. Yet in the bitter warfare back in Kentucky, by craft, by cunning guile, by the subtlety and the silence of Indians, by gathering in numbers and striking at few, the Dikkon clan had beaten down his own, harried them out of the country, sent them almost beggars into the West.

Then, with deathless malevolence, they had followed, and once more the Quinces were ruined. It was something like the story of Hydra—and, when one head of a Dikkon was cut off, two new ones came to take its place. Where he had killed some famous fighting man of the Dikkon name, two stalwart sons now were growing to maturity, seasoning their hatred for him and practicing with their guns. For nearly fifteen years no target had seemed worthwhile to any Dikkon save the target of the living Barney Quince. All his wounds of knife and bullet burned in him and printed their pattern anew with an electric tingle.

He went straight down the middle of the central street. There were lights in the hotel and saddled horses standing in front of it—no doubt a late game of poker was dragging on there. The long rays gleamed upon him as he went past. He felt the lightness of his empty Colt. Still he did not dodge into the shadows—skulkers are the first seen and the first shot at.

He came before a big store, calmly turned the corner of the building, and at a side window he tried his hand power. The window was latched, but the latch was weak and rusted. It gave with a sudden snap and squeak under the pressure and slid up. He waited, his head canted toward the ground, but he heard no sound.

He slipped through the window and carefully closed it again. It was pitch dark inside the room, so he lighted a match and, by its first glare, he scanned the nearby counters and the loaded shelves behind him. Clothes—but he could attend to clothes and shoes later on. What he wanted now were guns and ammunition, and he began weaving back and forth among the counters straight to the far end of the store. There he laid his hand upon a barrel of cold steel.

He stopped and straightened, struck with a sudden wonder. Surely he never before had been in that store. How did it chance, then, that he found the gun racks? These were the rifles. Then where were the revolvers? In his mind a picture seemed to rise—the revolvers were ranged on a rack just opposite, behind his back. He turned, groping in the dark, and laid his hands instantly upon them. Sweat stood on the forehead of Barney Quince. It was, indeed, as though some ghostly voice had guided him and guided him aright.

Ammunition, then? Well, try the second counter over to the

right and under it in cases. His hands were instantly upon the boxes. He loaded the two new Colts—he was so perfectly familiar with the weapons that he could take them apart and assemble them in utter darkness—and then he searched for a cartridge belt—two rows of pockets in it, the lower for rifle cartridges, the upper for revolver. Somehow he knew that he had seen them lying on a counter—yes, just behind the ammunition layout. There, indeed, they were. He filled the belt. He gathered up his revolvers, and the comfortable length of the rifle, and went to the clothing department again.

He had more difficulty there, and he had to risk the lighting of a dozen matches before he had found what fitted him. Shoes were even a greater labor. The lapse of time began to tell upon him, and the nerve strain made his hands tremble. But he was equipped from head to foot at the end of an hour. Slicker, boots, underwear, socks, shirts, a pair of good blankets, a Stetson, some silk bandannas, and the guns. He went back to the other counter and dropped some extra cartridges into his pockets. One never could have too many. Then he heard the noise of a key fitted ever so quietly into the lock of the door.

The new and heavy boots made no difference to him. Silently he stole across the store and shoved up the window without a noise equal to a whisper.

"Who's there?" called a frightened voice.

Gun poised, he turned. He heard a stumble and a faint curse in the distance. Some nerveless watchman had seen, or thought he had seen, the flare of one of the matches that Barney Quince had lighted. Now, like a fool that holds a lantern for his enemy to shoot by he came, announcing his coming. But Quince was already through the window and standing safely on the ground outside when there was a flare as the big gasoline lamp of the store was lighted. He peered in and saw the poor watchman crouched, his rifle at the ready, peering around him at the shadows and apparently frightened almost to death.

Barney turned away with a chuckle and started to return to Christie. But the way was to be longer than he had planned.

Chapter Ten
A Silent Struggle

As he reached the back yard of the store, he heard the double explosion of two shots fired in rapid succession from the interior of the big building. A window slammed wide, and a voice shouted loudly into the night: "Robbery! Thieves! Help! Help!"

Barney swung himself up to the top of the board fence and hung there, regardless of the dangerously clear silhouette which he cast against the stars for any watcher, any chance prowler. He waited, listening eagerly for the result of his mischief-making to become apparent. Presently there were answers from up and down the street and almost at once the spatting of rapid hoofs in the dust. No doubt the gamblers at the hotel had responded to the call. Windows began to open, and doors were slammed. He heard distinctly fragments of conversation as men strode up the street, and he heard deep cursings. The men of Adare seemed incredulous. It was not possible in their eyes that any man should dare to invade their precincts, their innermost circle, to plunder.

Very clearly he heard one prophet cry out: "If it's anyone, it's Barney Quince! It's him, come back to cover his nakedness!"

Barney dropped down on the farther side of the fence and jogged comfortably on down the line of back yards. He was passing a vine-covered stretch of wire netting when he heard the crunch of footfalls, too soft and light to be more than half guessed at and, before he himself could swerve, a man of Adare swung around the corner. They were so close to one another that Barney had not even time to whip out a gun. Instead, he darted a long left into the face of the man and then chopped a heavy right-hander on his jaw.

After that, he slipped back a little to give the man room to fall, since fall he must—for nothing living and calling itself human, surely, could resist two blows from the fists of Barney Quince. The other fell, decidedly, but he fell inwards and cast his arms around Barney as though to support himself. He was a Dikkon. Barney could be certain of that by the silence and the malevolence of the fellow's fighting. He was not tall. There was no giant in the clan. But the man was exceedingly broad and, when he fell against Barney's chest, it was as though a pillar of iron had dropped against the taller man.

Then the thick, slow arms of the unknown man moved around Barney Quince. He found that his left arm was bound against his side by the encircling pressure. The other arm of the stranger was biting into his ribs. There seemed literally no end to the strength of the man. He kept throwing in fresh power until Barney felt the wind going from his great chest. He knew with a sense of terror and of awe that for once in his life he was overmatched in sheer, Herculean strength.

His right arm was only partially imprisoned. He managed to tear it free and, then poising it, he struck. The trip hammer does not need to fall far, and neither did the leaden fist of Barney Quince. Twice and again he let it fall on the face of the squat man, and three times he felt his knuckles bite deep and jar against bone. But the man did not stir. He merely freshened his grip with a might that threatened to crush Barney's spinal column.

The latter changed his aim and, drawing back that lethal weapon, his right hand, he drove it home behind the ear of the stranger. The latter slackened his hold. One thrust and Barney was away from him, but still the enemy, though staggered, had not given up the battle. As a bulldog, having lost a grip, waddles steadily, resolutely in toward his foe, so this vast, squat, ape-like creature came waddling toward Barney Quince.

Something like fear came into the proud heart of Barney then, for half a dozen times he had smitten this fellow, and still the man had not gone down. He was almost tempted to draw a gun and fire, but he saw that his assailant, as though stunned, thought of nothing but hand-to-hand combat, and Barney Quince disdained to refuse a meeting on any grounds to any foe.

He fell back a little from the silent advance. Stepping in, deftly and lightly, he brought to bear the full weight of his body and the full smash of his active arm and wrist—and felt his hand jar home on that spot known as the button. Solidly and with all his strength he smashed. It was almost like hitting a rock. There was merely a small sagging of the head of this monster, while the half-broken hand of Barney Quince dropped back to his side.

It was unreal and ghastly. Quince felt his blood turn cold with the awful conviction that this could be no man after all, but some vast and horrible gorilla which presently would leap on him and bury its fangs in his throat. For still the monster did not fall but slowly waddled toward him, extending his arms like something without sight, feeling octopus-like for his prey. Wild terror arose in Barney Quince. He could, of course, whip out a gun and end the struggle with one well-planted shot, and against this beast-like creature he felt that gun powder alone should be used. Yet, doubtless, it was a man, and like a man it should be battled. So, his heart in his throat, he plunged swiftly in again, his teeth set and his eye narrowed.

His right arm dangled almost uselessly at his side, so terribly had the shock of the full stroke numbed it to the shoulder, but with the left he was well-nigh as strong, and with the left he smote now to the full of his power. Once again there was the true finding of the jawbone; and once more there was a shock as though beating against a house timber. Quince's numbed arms swung idly, foolishly at his side. He hardly could have drawn a weapon now if he had tried, and certainly he could have struck no mark with any gun.

So, scorning to fly, he stood before the squat shape. Indeed wonder and horror made it quite impossible for him to move from his place. A hundred times before, in his adventurous youth and in his manhood, he had fought with his bare hands, whether wrestling, or rough-and-tumble such as the miners delight in, or else standing off and fairly squaring away at an antagonist. In all those years, since he was a half-grown youngster, he had not known the man, no matter how vast of bulk, who could retain his senses after being struck fairly on the jaw by his fist. Yet here was one who had withstood two such blows as never before had he dealt—blows which he felt must have crushed the heads of normal men.

Half a dozen mortal seconds that squat bulk stood before him, its arms still outstretched, but its advance ended. It seemed more terrible than all else to Barney Quince that the figure made no outcry, no shout for help but simply stood uncertain. Then slowly, heavily, down upon one knee it slumped, both ape-like arms fell and supported it, and Barney Quince could see that the whole bulk was wavering a little from side to side.

The second punch, then, had told the story but, with a true fighting instinct, the stranger had still presented himself as if for battle. Barney hesitated. If he went on, this colossus might arise and follow him. If he remained long, he would have to resume the battle. There was nothing that Barney Quince wanted less than to taste the power of those arms a second time.

He jerked out a gun, for a tap with the long barrel of the Colt might be decisive. But he found that the weapon hung in air. It is no easy thing to strike a helpless man. So he turned away and ran straight toward the nearest trees—but then changed course at sharp angles behind the screen of them and hurried down the line of the village houses, anxious now to get back to Christie, where that good mare waited for him, still without a saddle. He cut in closer to the houses.

There was no such uproar as he had expected after the robbery was discovered. Instead, the people of Adare appeared to be returning to their houses. Only, in the distance and scattering here and there, Barney Quince made out the separate poundings of many riders, as they went on their way through the night. He was pleased by this. In all things the Dikkon clan worked sensibly, quietly, never making a vast uproar. Indeed, they were efficient men, efficient fighters. Though his blood boiled at the thought that they should have destroyed another clan of such men as himself, still he knew that there was a mighty force in them. Often it is easier for a hundred men to beat a hundred than it is for them to beat one. At least, one mounted on such a creature as the mare, Christie!

He dipped back toward the line of the houses, bent upon gaining a saddle fit for the mare. The first place that caught his eye was discarded for the sake of the second which was now made out against the stars in the near distance. He examined it as he came up with an odd feeling, as though he had seen it before.

As he came closer and saw the peculiar sway in the back of the barn, he told himself that this had been observed long before. Yes, he could swear to it. To the right and below that sway, on this side of the roof, there was a broad patch of new, unpainted shingles. Would that he had the daylight now to test the truth of what he had guessed. With his hand on a corral fence, he bowed his head and let his half-wakened memory work.

Down at the left hand was the granary—then the great barn with the work horses ranged upon the one side and the mules upon the other. There on the right was the feed shed for the winter cattle, when they were kept up, and for the milch cows. That smaller structure was the creamery where the flat tin pans stood in long, waiting rows. And yonder, above the trees, arose the pointed roof of the house itself. Beneath that roof was some delightful, some wonderful, some heart-devouring thing of beauty! What could it be? On that point his mind was blank.

Chapter Eleven
What Was It?

Like some creature that cannot see but is drawn on by another sense, like that of scent, Quince drew nearer to the house. It was very dangerous, he knew, to linger too long close to the village of Adare, now that it had been roused against him, but he could not resist the temptation. It forced him back from the barn, through the rear gate of the yard, and through the narrow path that pierced the vegetable garden.

He found himself taking the close turns by instinct, as though this were a place long familiar to him. Again and again he paused and tried to shake from him the impulse which urged him on, and still he was forced ahead with an invincible power that led him under the edge of the outhouses which lay behind the main buildings, across the soft lawn, and so beneath a window outside of which was a little balcony overhung with a vine. He knew that vine was starred with small pink blossoms as clearly as though the sun now shone upon it, and the sweet fragrance was also familiar to him. With every breath of that perfume the emotion drew deeper into his very soul, and he stared at the open window above him as a thief might stare at the entrance to a king's treasury.

It was not wealth of money that lay within. What it was, indeed, Barney Quince could not tell himself, but he actually laid hold upon the stout stem of the vine as though about to venture up the stalk. Then reason overcame the emotion. He forced himself back from that house with a reeling brain, telling himself that he was turning mad indeed. For what could lie inside the house of any Dikkon except hatred for him, guns prepared, and bullets straightly aimed?

He made a little detour, driving himself ahead, but every step he took away from the house was a step of pain. Still he made reason command him, and so he reached the next premises, and there he searched for a saddle and the proper equipment for Christie. He found it with the same unerring prescience which seemed to give him sight in the dark.

He passed the barn and went to a little adjoining shed, opened the unlocked door, and found within a range of saddles. He selected one that suited his purpose, took blanket, bridle, and all necessities. With the considerable burden he started back toward the spot where, so long ago, he had left the mare. It required skulking across the main street, but this he ventured over safely with not a sound or a sight to alarm him. He came eventually close to the little poplar copse where Christie should be.

Nearby, he flattened himself against the ground and listened. For the ground is a sounding board which sends out vibrations more distinctly than the thin air. Yet he heard not a sound except a faint gritting and grinding, and he took that to be the mare grazing quietly in her small preserve. He stalked closer, on hands and knees, thrusting his new rifle before him, when suddenly the tall form of Christie appeared out of the wood, and she whinnied to him in a whisper.

Very glad was Barney Quince to spring up and throw the saddle on her back, while she sniffed at his new clothes and tried to nip them away, to get at the man she knew beneath them. He made wild haste, for it seemed to him that he had been wandering through a region of ghosts and that the instincts which had been guiding him were such promptings as witchcraft, say, brings to light in the heart of a man. Badly frightened indeed, he could not recall ever having been so happy as when at last he could leap into the saddle and thrust his feet into the stirrups. He cast one wild glance around him and then headed Christie for the open ground.

He had half feared that the new burden might clog her speed, but he was reassured by the first stride she made. She floated away with him and all his equipment as though the whole were thistledown and she a wind to carry it. Then the wide valley received them, and the stretching darkness lay deep and thick between them and the lights of Adare. He drew her back now to a soft trot, and still he rode with his face toward the village, for a strange debate was raging in him.

Reason, sternly and steadily, told him that Adare was thronged with enemies who would laugh as they killed him, as dogs pull down a wolf. Yet that blind, strange instinct with a powerful hand checked him and almost turned him back, seeming to say in the clearest of voices that behind him, in Adare, a treasure beyond counting waited for him, a treasure that was neither gold nor horseflesh nor weapons. What it was then he could not imagine, but he knew that his heart leaped wildly, and a frantic joy took him by the throat. It was as though he rode on some lofty and dizzy mountain ledge and were tempted to fling himself into the air, assured that wings would bear him up and carry him swiftly over the white summits beyond. That temptation raged like a fever in his blood, and yet common sense told him that such a flight was terrible, unavoidable death.

At last he turned a resolute head to the front, and yet in five minutes he had turned again and brought Christie to a halt to stare at the dwindling rays of light that shone out and reached after him like hands through the darkness. Desperately, he gave Christie his heel and, while she rushed at full speed ahead, he set his teeth and closed his eyes. When he opened them again and glanced over his shoulder, all was darkness around him. He was in the silent heart of the desert with the feeling that he had escaped from fate. He had carried off a full accouterment at the expense of aching ribs where those terrible arms of the stranger in the dark had crushed him. Rarely had there been a more profitable and easy adventure.

Yet Quince was not at rest, for he told himself that fate,

after all, cannot be avoided. If he dared to question his heart, it told him that surely, before many days had passed, he would be led back blindly to Adare—and to what awaiting him?

By the stars and by the dim front of Mount Chisholm behind him, he laid his course with surety now and came at the end of two hours of easy travel to a small house between the glimmering face of a great tank on one side and the shadowy bulk of a string of cottonwoods on the other. Behind the house was a ragged line of sheds and a tangle of corrals, but all was on a small scale, so that even in the night the house seemed a pitiable thing, scarcely able to endure the withering heat of the sun and the sweep of the winter winds. He went to the front door and kicked heavily against it three times. He reined back and waited. Almost at once, a voice called from an upper window.

"Who's with you, Hilary?" asked Barney Quince.

"Hey, Barney," shouted the man of the house. "I thought we'd never have the luck to see you again. It's all safe here. Nobody but me and the girl. Feed your horse in the shed. I'll be down. . . ." As he turned from the window his voice was heard more dimly calling: "Marjorie! Marjorie! Hey, wake up! It's Barney come back to us!"

It soothed the puzzled heart of Barney Quince to hear this cheerful welcome. He fed Christie in the barn, and then he came back to find Hilary Clarkson hurrying toward him in the starlight.

His hand was wrung. He was led by the arm into the house, and there was pretty Marjorie, her eyes dancing, her nose a little more freckled than ever, dressed in a blue gingham wrapper. She gave him both her hands—which is *not* the Western way!—and then she made a tremendous racket at the stove and half filled the air with dust as she shook the ashes from the grate. Immediately the fire was blazing, the coffee pot was on, the frying pan began to smoke—as, with lightning hands, a place was laid on the clean oilcloth which covered the table.

"She's great, ain't she?" said Barney Quince in admiration

to the father. "What a woman she's turning out, Hilary!"

"Tell it to her," grinned the father. "She'll listen to you . . . maybe. Now lemme hear about yourself . . . and what happened to you, Barney, in Adare?"

But a shadow fell over the mind of the guest at that word. He set his jaw and frowned. Then he shook his head and made answer: "I'll talk about anything else. I don't want to talk about that."

"Hey?" cried Clarkson. "But smashing your way right through the whole mob of them . . . and getting clean off, bareback, on Steve Dikkon's best horse! The finest mare, they say, that ever stepped inside of Adare. Man, you mean you won't talk about that?"

"I'll talk about that," said Barney slowly, "but nothing else about Adare . . . it makes me a little sick, Hilary. I ain't myself. My nerves are turning upside down . . . and I dunno what's wrong with me."

The rancher nodded sympathetically.

"You take the life that you've been leading, and everything that's happened to you lately"—here he touched the back of his head and nodded significantly—"and it's sure to upset you some way. I tell you what, Barney, there's only one thing for you to do."

"Well, lemme hear?"

"It's simple and plain as the nose on your face. Change your name. Go north. Go somewhere on the range where nobody ever has seen your face. Start life over again, dead quiet . . . and ask a woman to be your wife . . . one that ain't afraid to rough it with you."

"Ah?" cried Barney Quince. "A woman? A woman?"

There was such a strange note in his voice that the girl by the stove started and then bowed closer over her cookery, a deep crimson flooding her face. But Barney Quince was looking far off at his thoughts, and he saw nothing that lived in that room.

Chapter Twelve
Pursued!

Now, in the dark of the room which was assigned to him, he sat at the window and looked across the plain, wide and level as a sea. These faithful friends, he knew, would watch over him and guard him like a member of their family. He could remain here safely until the next evening, when again there would be danger that the pursuit from Adare, passing out from that village in increasingly great circles, might reach as far as this. Yet safety from the pursuit of his enemies was not his concern. Safety from the assault of his own mad impulse was what haunted him.

For still he could breathe the fragrance of that shower of unseen bloom beneath the window of the unknown house in Adare, and still the memory of that perfume went into his mind like the rarest wine, and the house itself rose before the eye of his imagination, like something not once but a thousand times seen. Yes, it seemed to him that he could have opened the side door—he knew well that the key was kept beneath the mat—and he could have passed silently, even in the darkness, from hall to hall until he came opposite the door of that same chamber whose window he had stood beneath.

He buried his face in his hands, for the mere thought of the door, like the memory of the window, made his pulse leap wildly. It was only by a vast effort of the will that he was enabled to force himself into his bed. There he lay face down, his arms wrapped around his head to shut out the world of sight, the world of sound, the world of all imaginings.

He slept at last but a wild and broken sleep in which he

dreamed that he dreamed, and the dream became reality, and reality became the dream, so that he sat up in the morning, pale, faint, with a heart that fluttered weakly in his breast, as though he had been climbing mountains all night long.

Marjorie was already up and at work in the kitchen. She gave him a smile from an open heart, but he walked past her with a nod and went to the barn. On the way he passed Clarkson, who hailed him cheerfully. Christie, at least, would be something actual, a sunlight reality. No, when he saw her, though she filled his eye as a perfect mount, he could not help remembering that he had won her from the semi-fabulous town of Adare. Therefore, she was a part of the dream, she was the ever-present link that connected him with the past! How had he come by her? Where would she bear him? Back, of course, to the town. Back until he stood once more beneath that fascinating and dangerous casement, clad with vines and with immortal fragrance.

Barney Quince felt his brain reeling. He harnessed the mare. The saddle was in his hand when he knew what he must do, and he hurried out to find Clarkson milking his one cow.

"Hilary," he said, "have you got a pony here?"

"You mean something to carry you?"

"Yes."

"I was in and looked at the mare you borrowed from Steve Dikkon," grinned the rancher, "and you'll never need a second while you've got her to carry you."

"I want to change with you," declared Barney Quince. "I'll trade her for any good mustang that can pack me through a day's march."

Hilary stared. "I wouldn't have enough cash in a year's income," he said, "to pay you the boot you'd need."

"I want no boot," said Quince bitterly. "I'll give you the mare. You give me the mustang. We'll be quits."

Clarkson shook his honest head. "What I've done for you is too little, old man," he insisted. "You want to give me something. You ain't got the cash, so you offer me your horse.

Well, that's like you. But I couldn't take her. You don't owe me a thing. Why, Barney, you've always overpaid me.''

Barney Quince grew wroth. ''I tell you,'' he exclaimed, ''that all I want is to leave that mare behind me! I don't want her. I'm finished with her. She . . . I'd rather ride hellfire than ride her!''

The rancher stared again but with a vastly different expression. ''If that's really the way of it . . . well, there's my string in the little pasture. You go and take what you want.''

Barney Quince took a roan. It was a lump-headed creature, with little wicked eyes, but he felt that that humor would suit him exactly. So he packed that sturdy mustang, with the inward assurance that, if the little horse could not go fast, at least it could go far.

He returned to the house and, pausing near the door to scan the wide plain with a joyless eye, heard the rancher saying: ''I dunno what's wrong with him. He talks sort of crazy. It's the fall that he got, I suppose, and he'll never be the same man again!''

''Fall? No,'' said Marjorie, ''it's a woman. I know! When they get that wild, sad look . . . they're crazy about some girl. Poor Barney!''

Again, as on the night before, an electric shock leaped through the body and soul of Barney Quince. A woman! He felt as though a prophet had spoken out of a holy text; there could not have been more truth. There was a woman at the base of all his trouble. At the back of his brain, if he could make some vast effort, he would be able to visualize her features. It was the terrible and joyous hope of seeing her in the frame of the window above the balcony that had made his heart swell. It was the thought of her that had brought him to the door in the house of the stranger. Fate again! Yet, what a black curtain of uncertainty had fallen across his eyes.

He went in and had his breakfast and, when it was finished, he paused at the door, his quirt coiled in his hand, and leaned above pretty Marjorie.

"Marjorie," he said, "I heard you telling your father what's wrong with me. Are you sure of it?"

She, crimson, trembling, could not meet his eye, and her glance wavered from side to side. "I don't know, Barney," she managed to say. "I don't know . . . you ought to know . . . best . . . yourself."

"God bless me!" said Barney Quince. "Are you crying, really? Why? Look here, honey. The next time I come near a town, I'll find a present for you and bring it back."

The unbidden tears still streamed down her cheeks, but she clenched her hands and stamped. "I don't want your presents!" she cried at him.

Barney shrank awkwardly out of the house. He did not understand. Neither did he know, indeed, why Hilary Clarkson smiled grimly on one side of his face as he bade his celebrated guest adieu. But he was sure enough that all was not well between the family and himself.

He rode across the desert, aiming his course toward the pools which stand between Claverhouse Crossing and the Little Run. There he would water, rest his horse a day, and then start on through the real heat of the desert and its long, flat marches. He had only one direction in his mind and that was away from the town of Adare on the straightest line. He was putting between him leagues which, he felt confident, would blot from his mind the temptation which kept swelling there. He realized that Marjorie was right. He was in love and for the first time. In love with a nameless thing, a ghost, a thought, a nothingness.

Squaring his shoulders, he continued on the march, only turning now and again to scan the horizon behind him and all around. It was in one of those moments of observance that he saw a group of small black spots against the sky. He paused and looked at them with the greatest care. They gradually grew larger. He made sure by the rate of their approach that they were horsemen. With strange troops of riders he must take no chances, so he sent the mustang into a gallop and rocked steadily along over the loose sands.

For half an hour he kept up the pace and then looked back to make sure the four specks had disappeared. By no means! Instead of disappearing they had grown vastly larger, and he could distinguish them now without the slightest trouble. Four riders and undoubtedly mounted on blooded horses. Where could they come from except from the town of Adare? Who could be in those saddles except men of the clan of Dikkon?

Quince trimmed himself in the saddle and gathered in the slack of the reins. He worked the roan hard in a straight line ahead. Now and again he threw a backward glance. The roan was running hard and true, but the four were gaining with alarming rapidity.

What were those stories of mustangs capable of dropping behind them, in the uncertain footing and burning heat of the desert, all the well-bred horses of the world? Here was the chance to prove it, for the roan was a good one of his type, hardened by constant work, with every advantage except grain in his feeding. Yet he could not stand against these rushing riders on horses with a stroke that seemed twice as long as the bobbing roan's.

They drew nearer and nearer until Barney Quince unlimbered his rifle and calculated the distance for a long-range shot. Anger and scorn began to rise in him. For surely someone among them must have a pair of glasses—and they must know that they were riding in the pursuit of Barney Quince. Since when had four of the Dikkon clan dared to venture on the trail of Barney Quince?

Turning to view them more steadily, he saw that one was a strangely broad fellow. In the distance he seemed twice the size of any of his companions. Suddenly he knew by a certain premonition that this was his Hercules, his unknown warrior of the dark. A touch of coldness ran through the blood of

Barney Quince. Though why he should have felt fear he could not say. The odds, at least, were not enough to disturb him. Let them come within the range of his rifle, and quickly he would reduce their fighting force.

Chapter Thirteen
In a Circle

They came fearlessly on. He drew the mustang back to a soft canter and, turning in the saddle, he raised the rifle to his shoulder. At once the four split and spread out fanwise, though they made no effort to fire with their own weapons, frankly admitting that at such range they were helpless. Barney Quince was not helpless, and he fixed his grim eye on the squat and powerful form of his night foe. That man gone, the three would surely think twice before they pressed him closer. He stopped the mustang altogether, covered his man, and drew the bead so firmly that he felt as if a line were drawn from the muzzle, arching through the air, leading the bullet to the mark.

The other three were weaving their horses two and fro as they galloped, but the squat form of the stranger drove straight on, disdaining such maneuvers. Barney Quince, feeling in his heart respect for such dauntless courage, pressed the trigger and lowered his rifle to watch the fall. But the man did not fall. He rode on, and the wind curled and uncurled the brim of his wide sombrero.

Quince, stunned, blinded, was sure that the four could not be other than an empty mirage, still galloping closer, for it was not his wont to miss a human target. With an oath, he jerked the rifle once more into the hollow of his shoulder, took aim even more carefully—and at a target how much nearer?— then fired a second time. But still the squat and mighty horseman drove on, disdaining to weave from side to side, disdaining to draw his rifle for an answering shot, though his three companions had their weapons out now and were pumping a shower of lead at their foe. Barney was agape, half unnerved.

They were near enough now for him to see them turn in their saddles and point to the side and, following the gesture, he saw yet another rider sweeping over the sands, far swifter than the others. No, not a horseman, but a riderless horse which ran valiantly. The four swept to one side, waving their hats, shouting, as though they wished to cut off the advance of the strange horse. They might as well have striven with a thunderbolt for, arching out a little from the straight line of its coming, with the sun flashing on its polished flank, the great runner came for Barney Quince, and suddenly he understood. It was Christie, broken away from her new keeper and coming for her real master. Somewhere in the past he had heard of horses able to work out a trail—and no doubt she had seen the direction of his going. Here, at least, was the miracle sweeping toward him and the four riders hot behind her. He turned the mustang and rode with red spurs, as fast as the short legs of the sweating horse would carry him. But the whinny of Christie was coming up behind, and soon her shadow shot over the sand beside him.

The four were hopelessly distanced by her, but still they gained fast on the mustang, and Christie began to circle around her master in great loops, her ears flattened, curvetting high as though she threatened to dash the life from the mustang in one of those charges of hers. So Barney Quince, to take a gift that had fallen from the sky, undid the throat latch, undid the girths and, as they were dangling, he jerked the mustang to a halt, tore off saddle and bridle, and flung them on the mare.

The four behind knew well what that meant. They had their guns out, even the squat and formidable warrior. They clipped the air about the ears of Barney Quince as he jerked the girths up and then flung himself into the saddle. Let them ride their best, for Christie was away like a happy arrow driven toward a mark of its own seeking, and in the saddle Barney Quince turned and dropped a pursuing horse with his first shot. The rider rolled headlong, then got up staggering in a cloud of dust, and in another moment the remaining three drew rein, dropped from their saddles to the ground, and opened fire. The very first bullet cut through the crown of Barney Quince's hat, but luck favored him. Before him opened a draw just deep enough to swallow horse and man from sight and, dipping into it, in five minutes he was safely out of range.

He came back to the upper level and, looking to the rear, he could see the enemy gathered in a group as for consultation. With that, he put them from his mind. They had done their best, and their best was very good but not good enough for Christie.

He reached the water holes in the middle of the afternoon and gave the mare to drink. Then he rode on and made dry camp that night in a belt of greasewood that ran out down a shallow draw, creeping like smoke on the face of the desert. It was the loneliest night in all the life of Barney Quince. For in the other days—save long, long ago when his father lived—there had been no human interest in this world for Barney. Even that father had been rather more of a name than a flesh-and-blood reality. He had been seen by flashes, coming and going, save on a few occasions when he returned wounded and sick. The great work was all that occupied the mind of Barney's father—that great work of stinging the Dikkon clan like a gadfly, to madden them if he could not destroy them. In turn, Barney himself inherited the labor of his kind and made the feud a greater thing than happiness. For happiness, indeed, was only on the Dikkon trail, gun in hand. The record of his glory was the number of notches which he was entitled to file into the butt of his gun.

That was what humanity meant to him—gun fodder! There were, to be sure, certain so-called friends who were scattered here and there through the mountains and the desert. He had bought their kindness, and Hilary Clarkson was the best of them. But even Hilary, Quince well knew, could not be trusted past a certain point. His price could soon be reached.

There was no real tie between this wanderer and the whole human race. He looked upon himself not as a man, indeed, but as a highly perfected instrument of vengeance, and there was never a time when he would not gladly have laid down his life to take half a dozen lives of the Dikkon clan. However, there was another responsibility before him, for he must not only strike in person, but also he must leave another behind him to strike and to bear the name which he had borne. So one day he must have a wife—he looked forward to marriage as a necessary evil, a vast evil, and a trouble.

He who has no friends, and wants none, cannot be alone. But now it seemed to poor Barney, as he lay in the black hollow of the night, that one half of his soul was gone from him and stood again beneath the window of the house of the stranger in Adare. If there were a woman, a Dikkon she must be, and how could he exchange so much as a kind word with one of that infernal breed? Yet there was a pain in his heart, aching like an old wound in cold weather until he sat up with a groan, and Christie came softly toward him and snuffed loudly at his face.

He fell back again and closed his eyes to shut out the brightness of the stars, for they too were a part and a portion of the enigma in which he found himself. The world was strange to him, but far more strange than the world was the riddle of his own new-found soul. Fate, he was sure, had taken him in her hand. All things served to show it. No doubt what fate meant was that he should fall soon at the hands of the clansmen. For that matter from his earliest boyhood he never had conceived any other end as possible, proper, or desirable. He merely had hoped to extend the blood trail through many years. Now he knew that that trail was drawing to a close.

All things pointed to it. Men have premonitions before the end. So had he. Odd things begin to happen as a stormy life draws toward the final port. Lights glimmer from the unseen shore. So with him. With invisible noose he was drawn back toward Adare. Here was the mare from which he had separated himself now, as it were, by a miracle restored to him. Above all, there were those strange encounters with the unknown warrior who had wrestled with him in the dark, who had pursued him, and had been immune before his bullets.

The eyes of Barney Quince closed a little before daybreak, but his sleep was short and troubled. When he wakened, he rose with the gloomy air of a man who knows not where or to whom to turn. Like one who throws all burden upon chance, he let Christie take the lead that day and would go whithersoever she would, and very glad was he that she had turned away from Adare. He let her journey on, and he was gladder still when he lost his bearings altogether, for it was a pleasant relief to cast himself upon the broad shoulders of his fate. Let it guide him where it would.

A dust storm struck them in the afternoon and gave horse and rider three wretched hours, but Christie kept steadily on, dog-trotting with a stride that made the miles drift by. The wind fell, but now the sky was overcast, and the air still so filled with unsettled particles that it was like a dense fog through which the traveler could not see a half mile in any direction.

Darkness began, and the visibility became less and less, while Christie moved cheerfully on her self-appointed course. At last, at the top of an upgrade, in the middle of a pleasant wood, Quince made his halt for the night. In this darkness he could risk a fire with little chance of being seen, but no sooner had the flame begun to take in the wood than he looked up and saw the clouds widely parting across the arch of the stars, and then a changing wind began to clear the lower air. With haste he put out the fire and scattered earth carefully over the embers. He went to the edge of his little grove to look over the countryside and gain his bearings if he could.

Straight before him rose the mass of Mount Chisholm, with its familiar square shoulder, and in the valley beneath was a huddle of gleaming lights. Christie, swinging through a great circle, had brought him fairly back upon Adare!

Chapter Fourteen
Jim Dikkon

All that Barney Quince had dreaded before now he knew to be the truth, and the destiny against which he had vainly fought now overmastered him. The very animal which had come into his hands and which loved him was now an instrument which brought him bodily back to his enemies. She had saved him twice only to destroy him in the end. In a cold despair he surrendered his last hope and prepared himself to die.

He would not go down to the enemy as a ragged vagabond at least. He stripped and bathed in the starlight in a little runlet of water. He shaved in the darkness, an operation to which he was long accustomed. Then he dressed, brushed his clothes with care, and rubbed up his boots. Finally, he rubbed down Christie, resaddled her, and rode to meet the destiny which had been hounding him.

On the way, he looked to his guns and made sure that every chamber was loaded. There were fifteen shots in the rifle. There were six apiece in the revolvers. A heavy knife hung in the front of his belt and, as he drew nearer to the lights of Adare, he merely asked of fate that he might be allowed to empty his guns and then to die knife in hand, working what harm he could before the last of the clan of Quince fell under the hands of their ancient enemies. Indeed, it seemed to him that it had long been pre-ordained that the clan of Dikkon should triumph over its foes.

Let come what might, he turned Christie along the back of the town until he was opposite the great outline of the barn which arose behind the house of mystery. In a thicket he left her, and for an instant leaned his head against her sinewy, silken-surfaced neck. Then he went straight toward the house.

Like a cat he walked, pausing now and again and staring through the darkness. But no trap seemed laid for him and, if he were walking upon his fate, at least the Dikkons seemed unaware of the good fortune that was about to come to them.

He crossed the fences and the gardens once more. He passed beneath the trees which made a cool belt of shadows around the place, and again it seemed to Barney Quince that he could name them in the darkness—here an oak, there an elm, and there a holly bush beside the wall. He went to them and touched their leaves and then shuddered as he realized that his guesses had been utterly correct.

A curtain was drawn up suddenly, and a column of light flared forth at him. Out of its path he leaped and crouched in the darkness, with two guns ready in his hands. This, surely, was the end.

But no, the window was raised, creaking a protest. The sound of the voices of men came clearly out to him. One was a deep, husky rumble; one was clear and pleasant of tone, so Quince approached stealthily and stood to listen by the window. When he cared to risk a glance, he could see their faces. He knew them both.

One was a man of middle age, with a brown, kindly, shrewd face which, Quince was sure, he had seen a thousand times before, though he could give it no name. But in some other incarnation, in some other life, by some division and rejoining of his spiritual being, in whatever mysterious manner, he had known that man, and the very sound of his voice, and the small white scar which flecked his right cheek.

He knew all this and besides he knew well the second partner in that conversation. Enormous of head, bull throated, with shoulders as wide as a door, this was that night-fighter who had closed with him and so nearly crushed the life from his body. This was that same rider who had followed him over the desert with such remorseless courage and made his shots fly wild.

All this great power was not his now. There was a neat white bandage around his head, and his body, when his coat fell open, seemed oddly bundled. He lay back in a big easy chair. His face was pale, and his eyes were sunken in deep hollows.

Indeed, the first word that Barney Quince heard referred to the condition of this arch-enemy, for the older man was saying urgently: "You'd better go to bed, my lad. You shouldn't be sitting up like this. You'd better turn in and rest. The doctor. . . ."

"I tried bed and couldn't stay there," said the rumbling voice. "I've got to be up and around. Besides, I'm only scratched not really hurt!"

"A slash along your head and a furrow down your ribs . . . is that nothing, Jim? By heaven, you touched hands with death a couple of times today, old fellow."

The other leaned backward in his chair, his face disturbed a little with pain as he stirred.

"He's beat me twice," he said slowly, staring before him with unseeing eyes. "I never thought I'd find the man that could do it. He's beat me twice!"

The older man was silent. Barney Quince, his heart far lighter, listened eagerly. For, after all, his bullets had not missed. Each of them had touched the target, and each of them would have turned back any other man than this.

"Twice?" said the first speaker slowly. "Twice, Jim?"

The big fellow pointed to one side of his face, swollen and discolored.

"You mean where you tripped and fell into the lumber pile, Jim?"

"It was no lumber pile."

"What? That night the thief. . . ."

"I met the thief."

"Do you mean it?"

85

"I met him. He was Barney Quince. I put my glass on him today, and I knew it was him. And then we came closer, and I was surer. I've never seen him before except in the night, but I knew the cut of him. It was Barney Quince, and he was the thief. We fought, and he got in the first blow . . . he had that advantage." He paused, his lips working a trifle and his big jaw muscles bulging. "Afterwards, I managed to close with him, and I got my arms around him. . . ." After another of those eloquent pauses, he added: "I've had my arms around men before, cousin, and I've worked through their strength, big and small, and had 'em turn to pulp. Well, I tried to break Quince in two, and I put more power into it than I'd ever tried to put into another thing. I had a reason to want him out of the way, for the minute I saw him loom in the dark, I knew that fate had put Barney Quince in my way, and if I got rid of him. . . ." He paused again, and then lifted his head and looked keenly upwards.

"I understand," said the other. He nodded in perfect sympathy.

The man continued: "I was putting out my full power on him, Cousin Oliver."

That name startled Barney Quince, for now he remembered it perfectly—once it had sounded in his ears. Oliver! Oliver Dikkon—a kind and a just man! How could he know both the name and the nature of this man?

"But it was like . . . ," continued Jim Dikkon, "it was like hugging a cask. The bones of my forearms ate into the ribs of him. They were like the ribs of a ship! But still I had trust that I'd break him down. Then he tore one hand free and beat it into my face three times, and three times it was like being hammered in the face with a maul. I laid my head on his shoulder, where he couldn't get at me and, at the same time, I felt his body begin to sag. I thanked heaven. I told myself that I had won. I had a flash, maybe, of how fine it would be to bring in that grand man a helpless prisoner. Taken by one man, eh?''

He stopped again to laugh bitterly.

"But he wasn't taken," continued the narrator. "He clubbed his fist. It was like a lump of iron, and he brought it in behind my ear. Well, it got him loose from me. Afterwards I tried to rush in, but he stood away and his fists were like cannon balls. They seemed to hit straight through my head. He dropped me and stunned me. That was the lumber pile I stumbled into, Cousin Oliver . . . Barney Quince!''

Down Oliver's face great beads of perspiration were rolling. "It was as near a thing as that, Jim!''

"Aye, it was.''

"But at least you got away from him. He didn't have a chance to use a gun on you.''

"I lay on my knees, sick and seein' nothing. He could have finished me then. With a gun . . . or a knife, maybe. Or he could have choked me. I was that soft.''

"It's not his way, after all," observed Oliver Dikkon. "Give the devil his due . . . he fights fairly.''

"He does," agreed the warrior. "There's no murder in him. I'll give him his due. That night he outfought me. Today he beat me again. Still I tell you that I have confidence, Cousin Oliver.''

"Would you meet him again, Jim?" asked his cousin curiously.

"I'd meet him again, and I will meet him again," replied Jim Dikkon. "I've got a sort of feeling about it. I'm gonna have him at my mercy, the way he's had me at his. And then. . . .'' His face grew savage.

"And then?" asked Oliver Dikkon, leaning forward in his chair.

"Why," began Jim savagely, "why I'd. . . .'' His voice trailed off but, rallying fiercely, he said: "I have reason enough for wanting him dead, I guess?''

His glance again flashed upwards, and again Oliver Dikkon nodded in understanding as he answered: "So have we all . . . reasons a little different from yours perhaps."

"And still," murmured Jim Dikkon, "I dunno . . . I dunno . . . somehow I don't see the end of it!"

Chapter Fifteen
Louise

It occurred to Barney Quince, as he stood by the window, that had a Dikkon been in his place at such a point of vantage with two of the clan's enemies helplessly seated before him, their moments of life would have been short indeed. But he was not tempted to assassination, for like his father before him his battles were straightforward struggles in the open.

But, however interesting might be the conversation between Oliver Dikkon and his companion, it was not to listen to talk that Barney Quince had ventured into this danger. He left the window and returned beneath that vine-hung balcony which had clung like an obsession in his thoughts for days. The window above was open, but all was black within, and yet it seemed to him that a transcendent joy poured out to him from above. He laid his hand on the stalk of the climbing vine. He tested its strength, and a shiver ran through the foliage above, but all held fast.

Softly as he could manage it, he began to climb, and he drew himself up little by little until his hand could grip the lower edge of the balcony. Then, swinging once or twice like a pendulum, he lifted his leg over the railing and presently stood on the little platform, stifling the sound of his breathing.

In the dark square of the window he saw a form of glimmering white, like a ghost it stood before Barney Quince, and like a spirit it called to his soul. He heard a frightened cry: "Who is there?"

He answered, half stunned with fear and wonder: "It's me . . . it's. . . ."

"Barney! Barney!" cried the voice of a girl, and he thought there was both terror and joy in it. "Oh, Barney, you've come back . . . why are you here?"

She came closer. She stood in the window so that the clear starlight fell on her face, and he could see her. He knew that he had seen her before. This was the lovely mystery which had remained within the room, this was the thing for which he had been brought back. It was the weight of awe that dropped upon his heart that made Barney fall upon his knees.

"Who are you?" said Barney Quince. "Who am I? And in the name of heaven have I ever seen you before? And where? Because my brain's spinning like a top!"

"I'm Louise Dikkon. Of course you've seen me a hundred times . . . when you were living here."

"Dikkon!" he breathed, and the name stabbed him with a dreadful pain. "Dikkon!"

She leaned from the window, drawing a dressing gown around her shoulders.

"Barney, do you remember at all?"

"I begin to. It's all in shadow. But I begin to remember . . . Lou!"

"What brought you here?" she asked of Barney.

"You!"

Her breath caught.

"They have ten armed men in the house, ready to start for you in the morning. They hate and they fear you, Barney, and if they found you here, I couldn't save you. Do you understand? You're standing over powder."

"A man has to die some day," he answered her gravely. "I can't keep on living forever, Lou. I've tried to ride away. I've had to come back. I've had to come back to you, Lou. I won't leave. If they find me . . . then let it be the finish. What finer place could I get to die?"

She stepped through the window and stood by him, and he rose, towering above her. She caught his great arms and shook them in nervous desperation.

"I mean what I've said. They'd shoot you down with no mercy! There's nothing on earth that they'd rather do . . . they hate you . . . except my father and me. They all hate you, Barney. They don't know your kindness and your gentleness. . . ."

"Kindness?" murmured Barney Quince, amazed. "Gentleness? Lord it ain't me that you've known but some other man."

"Don't speak," said the girl. "They'll hear you. They'll hear you even if you so much as whisper, I think. Jim Dikkon will hear. He's not like other men!"

"Who is Jim Dikkon?"

"The man you wounded today. Don't you know?"

"He's going to ride after me?"

"Yes, yes!"

"He came here to hunt me?"

"He came here to marry me, Barney."

"Aye," murmured Barney Quince, "I guessed there was a real reason why he needed killing."

A door slammed heavily somewhere in the house. Footsteps came up the hall and paused.

"Lou!"

At that, overcome with terror, she swayed into the arms of Barney and clung to him. He drew her closer and felt the warmth and tremor of her body.

"Lou!" called a voice from the hall.

Distinctly they heard another say more quietly: "She's sound asleep. Let her be, Cousin Oliver!"

The footsteps retreated.

"Go now!" gasped Lou Dikkon. "You see? Jim Dikkon suspects something, and he brought my father up to see if anything were wrong! He's like a hunting dog. His brain isn't like the brains of other people. Go now, Barney. In another minute it will be too late."

He leaned above her and kissed her forehead, and then her lips. When she tried to speak again, he kissed the words away. That fragrance which he had breathed before now entered his very soul never to leave it until his death day. She, faint and pale, swayed in his arms.

"Lou, if they were to find me now and kill me, I'd laugh as I died. Why do you try to send me away? It ain't the years a man lives that counts. All the rest of my life, compared with this, why, I'd chuck it away and laugh as I chucked it. It ain't worth thinking of. I tell you, Lou, heaven or the devil or something sent me back to you, and I'm helpless. I can't leave you!"

"Barney," said Lou, pushing herself back to look up into his face, "I know that you love me."

"Love is a fool word," said Barney Quince. "There ain't any word that could name what I feel for you, if you understand that."

"Barney, I know that I never can care for any other man. Even when your brain was stunned and you were so like a poor child, I loved you, but I didn't know it until the doctor took you away, and the operation...." Her voice failed.

"I'm beginning to understand things," said Barney Quince. "I'm only beginning to understand. This was where I stayed when I was out of my head."

"Yes, yes, yes!"

"And I lived right here among the Dikkons?"

"My father wouldn't let them hurt you. Afterwards ... I think everyone grew fond of you, Barney. Only when they knew that your were getting well and had forgotten everything here ... they tried to take you."

"I begin to see it. Your father kept me here?"

"More than eight months, Barney."

"If I'd met him afterwards, not knowing, I would have shot him down not thinking. I tell you, Lou, let them do what they want with me, because they've had me in their hands once, and I owe them a life. D'you understand?"

"But for my sake, Barney? Go away for me, because I do love you, dear! Will you listen to me? We can arrange places to meet ... and then something may happen so that we...."

"I stay here," he answered calmly, "because I know that I've come to the end of one life, Lou. I can count the seconds of it running away from me like blood . . . d'you think that I'll give up my time with you to spend it anywhere else?"

She said in desperation: "If you'll go, Barney . . . I'll do anything! I'll go with you. I'll stay with you. I'll live with you in the wilderness, Barney. Will you go now?"

"You go with me?" he said, holding her head in his great hand. "How would you live as I live, Lou?"

"I'd find a way. You and I together would find a way. I'm not the least afraid of that. I only know that if you stay here, they'll surely kill you. I'll never live after you're dead, Barney. I'll never live a day!"

He stood rigid.

"Me like a sneak and a thief," he murmured hoarsely, "stealing you away! But maybe this is the end of my old life and the beginning of the new life. I'll trust my chance to it and you, if you're willing to try. Lord knows . . . some way may turn up. Lou, go dress. I'll wait for you at the bottom of the balcony."

"I'll be there in one single minute."

"Good bye, dear."

He saw her vanish in the darkness of the room; then he swung lightly over the edge of the balcony and lowered himself, cautiously, carefully, to the ground. There he stood, looking up. She like a white flower would lean from the vine shower above him, before long. She, too, would climb down, and his arms would receive her. How plain it seemed to Barney that God directs all things in this world.

For a single instant a shadow crossed his mind. She was to him like an angel, with all the indescribable air of holy things about her, yet her name was Dikkon. She was of the enemy clan. If she became his wife, the long war would be ended. He could not raise his hand against her kindred and the blood relations of their children, if children came to them. So it would be, as he could see, the end of the old life, and the beginning of the new the instant that he received her in his arms.

Something, he thought, stirred softly behind him, and he was about to whirl, gun in hand, when an object was thrust sharply into the small of his back and a deep voice said in a subdued tone:

"Barney Quince, Barney Quince, say your prayer if you got a prayer to say, because you're dyin'. Barney, you're almost dead."

Chapter Sixteen
The End of the Feud

It would be folly to attempt to make any movement. Quince's hand closed on a tendril of the vine and crushed the delicate leaves to nothingness.

"You're Jim Dikkon?" he said.

"I'm Jim Dikkon."

"I should have killed you the first time I met you," said Barney Quince. "I was a fool . . . I was a rank fool!"

"I'd give you a fair fighting chance," said Dikkon, "except that there's the girl mixed up in this. You've got to die for her sake, man."

"I'll ask you for one thing."

"Well, ask."

"Walk me back into the trees and finish me there."

"Aye," murmured Jim Dikkon, "because otherwise she'd know who. . . ."

A whisper floated down from above: "Barney, Barney, darling!"

"Yes?" whispered Barney Quince. He raised his head and barely could see her.

"Are you ready for me?"

"Aye, ready."

"I'm coming down."

She slipped over the edge of the balcony, and Barney heard a faint murmur behind him: "Lord forgive me! Lord forgive me! *She* never will. . . ."

The reaching arms of Barney received the girl and held her closely to him. Only then she saw and turned rigid in his arms.

"I can't do it," said Jim Dikkon suddenly. "You ought to die Barney Quince, for her sake. But instead, if you'll go with her into the house and face her father and tell him what you would have done for her . . . do you understand?"

They sat in a family circle around the fireplace, though the hearth was black and empty. Oliver Dikkon had his daughter on one side of him, and Barney Quince sat on the other. In the background sat the captor, contributing no word to the discussion but keeping his burning eyes fixed solemnly upon the face of the enemy of his clan.

Oliver Dikkon said at last: "I had a sort of an idea of what might come the first night that we had you here. I had an idea," he went on, leaning as though he were watching a rising flame in the fireplace, "when I saw Lou caring for you. Because there's nothing that softens the heart of a woman like seeing an enemy helpless. Lou, here, isn't the sort that is apt to open her heart twice. Afterwards, I was pretty sure of it. All the time that you were here was a time of hell for me. I saw her growing to care about you. I couldn't send you away. I couldn't send her. She wouldn't have gone! You remember, Lou, when I wanted you to visit your aunt in Chicago?"

"I remember," she answered softly.

"Well, then the doctor came and did his work. It seems to me that heaven has taken charge of the rest. We've hunted Barney Quince with our best men. We never could take him or hold him. Jim nearly died on the trail today. If I go to the family council and ask them, face to face, if it isn't worthwhile to have you as a friend and the husband of my girl, I guess they'll rage and curse a little, but in the end they'll take you. Once you're in the clan, there'll never be a hand lifted against you by man or boy that wears the name of Dikkon. Jim, am I right?"

But Jim had stolen from the room.

Then, for the matter could not wait, Oliver Dikkon left the house to bring the family council together to decide this grave matter. Barney and Louise were left sitting, staring wide eyed at one another.

"I begin to remember, sort of," said Barney Quince, suddenly closing his eyes. "I remember a saw . . . a cross-cut saw, Lou, that you gave me to work with."

"Yes!"

"And the cows! And the hunting! And the woodchopping!"

"Barney, Barney, it's all coming back to you!"

"It looks to me," said Barney with the broadest of grins, "as though you'd been sort of training me for the job of husband, Lou, right from the start."

OUTCAST BREED

Outcast Breed

In 1920 Frederick Faust expanded the market for his fiction to include Street & Smith's *Western Story Magazine,* and his popularity there helped increase its circulation from a half million copies an issue to over two million. It was not unusual for him to have two serial installments and a short novel in a single issue under three different names. In 1934, Popular Publications agreed to buy 200,000 words by Max Brand, and this resulted in seven short novels published in *Star Western*, among them "Outcast Breed," appearing in the October, 1934 issue. It has since been issued by Audio Renaissance in a slightly abridged version read by Barry Corbin. For its inclusion here, the author's original version of the text, first published by the University of Nebraska Press in August, 1994 in *The Collected Stories of Max Brand* edited by Robert and Jane Easton, has been used.

Chapter One
Renegade Blood

Cameron saw the ears of the rabbit above the rock when he was a hundred yards away. He began to stalk with the care he might have used to get at a deer. Meat in even small portions was so valuable to him and Mark Wayland. As long as the rifle ammunition held out, they had fared well, but it is as hard to get within revolver-shot of desert game as it is to surprise a hawk in the naked sky.

Through the dusty film of twilight Cameron took aim and fired, not exactly at the ears but at the imagined head beneath them, hoping to break off the edge of the rock with the weight of his bullet. But the rock shed the speeding lead as it might have slanted a drop of water. Not one rabbit appeared, but three of them exploded from the shelter, and each ran in a different direction. Cameron stood up as tall as his toes would lift him. The olive darkness of his face and the brown of his eyes lighted. He smiled a little. It was hard to tell whether it were cruelty or joy or a sort of pity that inspired this smile. And then the revolver spoke to north, west, south, rapidly, the nose of it jerking at each explosion. The first two rabbits skidded along the earth, dead. The one to the south leaped high into the air and that pitiful, half-human shriek which only a stricken hare utters sounded to Cameron's ears. The pain of that jerked the head of Cameron to the side. Then his fifth shot accurately smashed the backbone of the jackrabbit from end to end.

Before Cameron moved again, halted as he was in mid-stride, he rapidly reloaded the Colt. It seemed a single, uninterrupted gesture that jammed the five cartridges into the chambers. When the cylinder was filled again, Cameron picked up the game, cleaned it, tied it in a bleeding bundle for the return trip, and then stood straight once more to scan the horizon. A fox or a wolf will do this after the flurry of the fight, when there is dead game to be eaten—a last look toward all possible danger before the feeding begins, and never a wolf had eyes brighter than those of Cameron.

It was during this rapid scanning of the whole circle of the twilight that he saw the glimmer on the head of the mountain, up there between the ears of the height where stood his and Wayland's mine. That trembling gleam could be but one thing—the shimmer of flame. The shack was on fire. In some way—it was inconceivable—Mark Wayland had permitted the cabin to become ignited. Once the fire caught on the wood— with no water available for the fight—there was nothing to do but shovel earth at the flames. And perhaps the fire would spread into the shaft and burn the timbers; the shaft would collapse; the labor of the many months would be undone, just as they were sinking into the valuable heart of the vein, just as they were writing the preface to a wealthy life, an easy future divorced from the need of labor, of sweat and worry.

Cameron, through the space needed for one long breath, thought of these things. Then he stripped the ragged shirt from his back, wrapped the precious meat in it, and, slinging the shirt around his shoulders like a knapsack, he began to run. He ran with his eye on the flame-spotted head of the mountain. As for the roughness of the terrain, his feet could see their own way. The half-Indian blood of his mother gave him that talent. Like an Indian, he toed in slightly, his body erect in spite of the weight on his back, his breathing deep and easy, an effortless spring in his stride. There was something of the deer about him, something of the predatory wild beast, also. He would catch his game, if not at the first spring, then by wearing it down. When it was caught, he would know how to kill. For if he had the body and the darkened skin of an Indian, he had the proud features of the white man, and the white man has always lived by blood.

When he came to the end of the valley, he started up the ascent of the trailless slope with a shortened step. The small weight of the rabbit meat was beginning to tell on him now. The burning of his lungs, the trembling exhaustion of effort, the agony of labor was stamped in the heaving for breath and in his shuddering belly-muscles, but it appeared only as a slight shadow on his face in the sweat that polished the bronze of his body.

So he came to the upper level, the head of the elevation where he and Mark Wayland had found the thin streak of color, long ago, and had begun their mine. He had brighter light than that of the dusk. It came from the ruins of the cabin, weltering with flame. And out of the throat of the mine shaft issued a boiling mist of flame and smoke. The cabin was gone. The labor on the shaft was ruined also. Well, all of this could be reformed, redone. They had the plunder that three weeks of work in the heart of the vein had put into their hands— fifty pounds of gold dust. Perhaps it would be wiser anyway to take the money to town, turn part of it into hired labor, tools, powder, mules, and return to reopen the mine with ten-fold more advantage.

He thought of that as he stood on the edge of the little plateau and saw the flames. The fire made little difference. But where was the figure that he had imagined hard at work, shoveling earth? Where was Mark Wayland? Where was that big, stocky body, that resolute face?

"Mark!" he shouted. "Mark! Oh, Mark!"

He had no answer. A dreadful surmise rushed into Cameron's mind, a sort of darkness, a storm across the soul. He ran forward past the mouth of the mine, past the crumbling, flame-eaten timbers of the hoist, toward the fiery shambles of the cabin. It had fallen in heaps. The fire was rotting the heaps away. Smoldering, charred logs lay here and there where they had rolled from the shack. A more irregular shape was stretched on the ground, smoking. He had passed it when something more profound than the sight of the eyes stopped him. He turned back to that twisted shape and leaned over the body of Mark Wayland.

Strong wires had been twisted around the arms, fastening them helplessly to the sides. The legs had been wired together at the knees and also at the ankles. There was a gag crammed into the mouth, distending it wide. Fire had eaten the body. Someone had come, caught Mark Wayland by surprise, robbed the cabin, bound the victim, and trusted to the fire to rub out the record of the crime. Then Cameron saw that the eyes of the man still showed life. A cry came from Cameron like the scream of a bird. He snatched the gag from Wayland's mouth. He picked up the great, smoking hulk of the body in his arms to carry it to the life-giving waters of the creek.

The voice of Wayland stopped him. The voice was calm. "I'm dead," he said. "I'm already in hell. Don't waste . . . motions. Listen to me."

Cameron laid his burden back on the ground. He broke the wires that bound the captive. With his bare hands he stopped the red coals of fire that ate at the clothes of the victim.

"A gray mustang," gasped Wayland. "He was riding a gray mustang with a lopped ear . . . lopped left ear. A big . . . man. . . . Gimme that gun."

"No, Mark!" shouted Cameron. "I'll take care of you. I'll make you well."

"God," gritted Wayland. "Don't you see that I'm burned to the bone? My face'll rub away like rot." Again he added, half-sobbing: "Gimme that gun. . . . A big kind of man . . . a gray mustang with a Roman nose and a lopped left ear. . . ."

"Mark, you've been a father . . . for God's sake let me be a son to you now. Let me try. . . ."

"Are you gonna show yourself a damned half-breed after all?" demanded Mark Wayland. "Gimme that gun."

Cameron was stiffened upright on his knees by the insult. He drew out the revolver and dropped it on the ground. He whirled to his feet and began to run. He realized that he could not run beyond the sound of the gunshot and cast himself down on his face, with his hands clasped over his ears. But he heard, nevertheless. It seemed as though the noise were conducted to him through the earth. His body drank it in not through the ears only, but through every nerve. It was a deep, short, hollow, barking noise. And it meant that Mark Wayland was dead. It meant that the years were struck away from Wayland. It meant the years he had spent in rearing and caring for the outcast Cameron could never be repaid, nor the patience in teaching that had endowed Cameron with far more than his preceptor had ever known.

The whole future was snatched away from Cameron, the whole chance of making a return to his benefactor. And all the love that he had poured out toward Wayland would now have no object. It would blow away in the wind. It would be wasted on a ghost. Cameron lay still on the ground. But there was one thing to live for. There was the man—the big sort of man who rode the gray mustang with a lopped left ear. Cameron got up from the earth as a cat rises from sleep at the scent of prey.

The trail could not be followed by night. Cameron spent the darkness in digging the grave. He carried to the grave the dead man with the flame-eaten body and the purple-rimmed hole in the right forehead. Into the pit he lowered the dead man. Over the body he first laid with his hollowed hands a layer of brush, because he could not endure the thought of rocks and earth pressing even on the dead face. Afterwards he filled the grave. He wanted some sort of ceremony. Instead, he could only give his own voice. And his own voice was too small for the moment. It could not fill the vast space of the mountains and the desert which the dawn was beginning to reveal. Therefore, as he kneeled by the grave, Cameron merely lifted to the morning in the east his empty hands and made a silent vow.

Afterwards, he took the revolver and went on the trail. There were only five bullets in that revolver now. But he had enough rabbit's meat to last him for a time. He followed the trail across the desert. It took him three days to get to the hills and to the town of Gallop. There the sign disappeared. But if he ever found the trail of that horse again, he would know it. He would know it by the length of the stride in walking, trotting, galloping. He would know it by the size of the hoof prints.

The only description he had of the rider was of a "big sort of man," and Gallop was filled with big sort of men. Therefore, he left the town and cut for sign in circles around it. Every day he made the circuit until at last, on the old desert trail, he found what he was looking for. He had not been able to spot the gray horse in Gallop, but he had found the trail of it, leading from the place.

Two days he ran down that trail, for the rider traveled fast. For two days the flesh melted from the body of Cameron as he struggled along the traces of the unknown. At the end of the second day, he saw a winking fire in a patch of mesquite beside an alkali water hole. He crawled to that fire on his belly, like a snake, and saw, standing nearby, eating from a nosebag, a gray mustang with a Roman nose—a dirty gray mustang with a yellow stain in the unspotted portion of its hide. And its left ear was lopped off an inch from the point. By the fire sat a big man with a broad, red face and red hair. When Cameron looked at him, he smiled and took a deep breath. The weariness of the two days of running slipped from his body. The tremor of exhaustion passed away from his nerves. His hands became quiet and sure. Then he stood up at the edge of the firelight.

"Put up your hands," said Cameron.

The red-faced man looked up with a laugh. "You won't get anything off of me except a hoss and a half a side of bacon, brother," he said. "What's the matter?"

"Stand up," commanded Cameron.

The red-faced man grunted. "Aw . . . well . . . ," he said. And he rose to his feet.

"You've got a gun on your hip," said Cameron. "Use it."

"What's the matter?" shouted the other. "My God, you ain't gonna murder me, are you?"

Fear rounded his eyes. He looked like a pig, soggy with fat for the market. A horror surged up in Cameron when he thought that this was the man who had killed Mark Wayland. As well conceive of a grizzly slain by a swine.

"Look," said Cameron, "I'll give you a fair chance. I'm putting my gun up, and we'll take an even start. . . ."

This chivalry was not wasted. The man who looked like a pig snatched his own weapon out, suddenly, and started fanning it at Cameron with the flick of a very expert thumb. He should have crashed at least one bullet through the brain of Cameron except that instinct was as keen as a wolf in him always. It told his feet what to do, and, as he side-stepped, he whipped out his own gun. If he could kill three scattering rabbits on the run, he could kill one red-faced swine that was standing still. Cameron drove a bullet for the middle of the breast. It clanged on metal instead of thudding like a fist against flesh. The revolver, jerked out of the fat fingers, was hurled back into the red face. The big fellow made two or three running steps backwards, gripped at the stars with both hands, and fell on his back.

Cameron picked up the fallen gun. It was whole.

"Here," he commanded. "Take up that gun, and we'll start again."

The other pushed himself up on his hands. There was a bump rising on his forehead, but otherwise he had not been hurt. "Who are you?"

"My name is Cameron. Stand up."

"I ain't gonna stand up. God Almighty saved my life once tonight, but he won't save it twice. Cameron, I never done you any harm. Why are you after me?"

"You've done me more harm than any other man can ever

107

do!'' exclaimed Cameron. He came a little closer, drawn by his anger. Hatred pulled the skin of his face taut. ''When you did your murder . . . when you wired him into a bundle and left him to burn in the cabin . . . you didn't know that he'd manage to wriggle out of the fire and live long enough to put me on your trail. But. . . .''

''Wired into a bundle . . . burn in the cabin . . . what are you talking about, Cameron? I never killed a man in my life.''

''What's your name?''

''Jess Cary.''

''Cary, tell me where you got the gray horse?''

''From Terry Wilson, back there in Gallop.''

''What sort of looking man is Wilson?''

''Big sort of feller.''

Surety that he was hearing the truth struck home in Cameron's brain like a bell-clapper against bronze. He began to tremble. It was as though God had indeed turned the bullet from the heart of Jess Cary, and only for that reason were the hands of Cameron clean. Back there in the town of Gallop—a big fellow by the name of Terry Wilson—a man who had been anxious to sell the gray horse—that was the murderer of Mark Wayland. Cameron backed off into the darkness.

Chapter Two
Killer's Track

He had a last picture of Jess Cary, glowering hopelessly after him from the small, ragged circle of the firelight. Then he turned and struck back through the night. There was big Terry Wilson to be reached. But Terry Wilson was a known name in Gallop, it appeared, and men whose names are known are easily found. Terry Wilson would have to die. Then some peace would come to the tormented ghost of Mark Wayland.

This thought soothed the soul of the hunter. During the last two days he had made great exertions, following the trail of Jess Cary. So, when he reached a run of water in the hills at the edge of the desert, he stopped the swinging dog trot with which he covered ground and lay down to rest. Infinite fatigue made the earth a soft bed. As for the hunger which consumed him, a notch taken up in his belt quieted that appetite. In a moment he was sound asleep.

He had five hours of rest by dawn. Fatigue still clouded his brain, so he stripped, swam in a pool of the stream, whipped the water from his brown body, and then ran in a circle until his skin was dry. After that, he dressed and ran on toward Gallop with the same effortless pace that always drifted him over the trail. A jackrabbit rose from nothingness and dissolved itself with speed. He tipped it over with a snap shot and ate half roasted meat, sitting on his heels at a hot, smokeless fire of dry twigs. Afterward, he lay flat for twenty minutes, sleeping. He then rose to run as lightly as ever toward Gallop. That night he slept three hours, ran on again, and entered Gallop in the early morning when life was beginning to stir. He had two bullets left in his gun, but two bullets would be enough.

The blacksmith had the doors of his shop open and was starting a fire in his forge.

"Terry Wilson . . . can you tell me where I can find him?" asked Cameron.

The blacksmith looked up from the gloom of the shop. "Terry Wilson. Sure. He's got the corral at the end of the town. He's the horse dealer."

The horse dealer. The lightness went out of Cameron's step as he turned away. He had thought that vengeance was about to fill his hand. Instead, it was probable that Wilson was only another milestone, pointing down the trail of the manhunt. He reached the corrals of the horse dealer in time to see a new herd driven through the gates of the largest enclosure. They washed around the lofty fences like water around the lip of a bowl. Dust rose in columns, a signal smoke against the sky. Dust spilled outwards in billows, and in that mist Cameron found a big fellow who was pointed out to him.

"Mister Wilson," he said, "you sold a lop-eared gray to Jess Cary, didn't you?"

The man turned his eye from the contemplation of the horses. "Jess stick you with that no-account mustang?" he asked.

"Where did you buy the gray?" asked Cameron.

"Tierney," answered Terry Wilson. "Will Tierney." His eye changed as he stared at Cameron. "Ain't you Mark Wayland's 'breed?" he demanded.

The question stiffened Cameron's spine to ice. Something broke in his brain, and a mist of red clouded his eyes. He had to force himself to turn on his heel, slowly, and walk away. It was not the first time he had heard the word. 'Breed, usually, or half-breed in full, from men with no friendliness for any part of Cameron's heritage was slurring him for life. Would it always to strike at him like poison in his shadow? And why? He could wish that he had not led such a secluded life with

Mark Wayland, riding, shooting, working as hard as any man, and then, in the evening, stretching out beside the campfire with one of Wayland's books. He knew something of grammar and books; he knew the wilderness; but he knew nothing of men. Of the human world he had had only a few score glimpses as he passed through with Mark Wayland. Now it seemed that the strange insult of the word 'breed was to be cast in his face from every side.

But why? His mother's mother had been a beauty of the Blackfoot tribe, a queen of her kind. Was there not honor in such blood? A chieftain of the frontier had married her. Was not their daughter able to hold up her head even before thrones? Three parts of his blood were white, and, as for the other part, he could see in it nothing but glory. Yet the world called him 'breed as it might have called him cur.

Will Tierney was asleep at the hotel.

"I'll go up and wake him," said Cameron.

"The hell you will," answered the hotel clerk. "He'll take your skin off if you wake him up before noon. Tierney ain't a gent to fool with. I guess you know that."

Cameron left the lobby. He could wait till noon, easily enough. Behind him his acute ear caught the phrase: "That's a 'breed, ain't it?"

"Yeah. Walks like one."

Why? What was the matter with his walk? Had Mark Wayland kept him purposely in the wilderness during those long prospecting trips so that his skin would be tough before he was exposed to the tongue of the world?

He found a tree in the little plaza opposite the hotel and sat on his heels to smoke a cigarette and think. Sun was filling the world. Over the roof of the hotel he could look up the gorge of Champion Creek and see the white dazzle of the cliffs on its western side. There was beauty and peace to be found, but, where white men moved in numbers, there was insult, cruelty. . . .

111

The morning wore away. The sun climbed. The heat increased. A magnificent fellow came down the steps of the hotel and strode along the street. There was a flash and a glory about him. He had that distinction of face that is recognized even at a distance. He bore himself with the pride of a champion. And if his blue silk shirt and silver conchos down his trousers and glint of Mexican wheel work around his sombrero made a rather gaudy effect, it would be forgiven as the sheen of a real splendor of nature. So that was Will Tierney? Cameron could have wished the name on a fellow of a different aspect, but nevertheless he would have to accost the handsome, swaggering giant. He was up and after him instantly, and followed him through the swing doors of Grady's Saloon on the corner. A dozen men were inside breathing the cool of the place and the aroma of beer and the sour of whiskey.

"Step up, boys," Tierney was saying. "Line up. It's on me."

A trampling of feet brought everyone toward the bar as Cameron stepped to the shoulder of Tierney and said, "Mister Tierney, you sold a lop-eared gray mustang to Terry Wilson. Do you mind telling me where you got the horse?"

Tierney turned with a sudden jerk. His upper lip pulled back in a sneer that showed the white of his teeth. His eyes were the black of a night that is polished by the stars. He gave to Cameron one glance and then nodded to the bartender.

"Grady," he said, "since when have you been letting 'breeds drink in your place?"

The bartender grunted as though he had been kicked in the stomach. "Is that a 'breed? By God, it is. Throw him out! Get out, you damned greaser."

A bowlegged cowpuncher with a bulldog face and neck shook a fist under Cameron's chin.

"That means you. Get," he growled.

Tierney stood back against the bar with one hand on his hip, the other dangling close to the butt of a revolver that was strapped to his thigh. He was laughing.

"You . . . Tierney . . . it's you that I want to talk to!" exclaimed Cameron. "Where did you get that gray horse? Will you answer me that? It's a fair question."

"Grady," said Tierney, "do I have to talk to the greasers you keep in your place?"

The cowpuncher with the face of a bulldog drove a big fist straight at the head of Cameron. His punch smote thin air as Cameron dodged—right into the sway of another powerful blow. There were a dozen enemies, all bearing down. He tried to shift through them. Hands caught at him. Fingers ground into his writhing flesh like blunt teeth. His gun was snatched away. A swinging Colt clipped the side of his head and half-stunned him. Then he was through the swinging doors. The sunlight along the street was like a river of white fire that flowed into his bewildered brain. Hands thrust him forward. He was kicked brutally from behind and pitched on face and hands into the burning dust of the street.

"Where's a whip?" called the clear, ringing voice of Tierney. "We'll put a quirt on the 'breed dog!"

A whiplash cut across the back of Cameron and brought him swiftly to his feet in time to take another lash across his shoulder and breast. Then a rider plunged between him and the Grady crowd.

The horse was skidded to a halt. A girl's voice shouted: "What a crew of cowards you are! A dozen of you on one man. A dozen of you. Will Tierney, isn't there any shame in you? Joe . . . Tom Culbert . . . Harry . . . I'll remember that you were all in this."

They scattered before her words as before bullets. Two or three hurried down the street. The rest streamed back through the swing doors of Grady's saloon. Their shouted laughter beat on Cameron's brain. He had dragged off his ragged hat and looked into the gray eyes and the brown, serious face of the girl. She wore a blouse of faded khaki, a well-battered divided riding skirt of the same material. But every inch of the horse she rode spoke of money. That was not what mattered. The thing she had done talked big in the mind of Cameron. And it seemed to him that he could look into the beauty of her face as far and as deep as into the loneliness of a summer evening in the mountains.

"It was rotten of them," the girl flared. "I don't care what you were doing . . . it's rotten for a dozen to pick on one man."

He put his hand over his shoulder and tentatively felt the welt the whiplash had left. It was still burning and growing. He could feel it easily through his shirt.

"I was asking a question of one of them, and they didn't want me in there. So"—he made a quick gesture—"they threw me out." As he said this, in trying to cover his expression of rage, he smiled.

"Ah?" said the girl. "The drunken hoodlums. I'm Jacqueline Peyton. Who are you?"

"John Cameron," he said.

"Cameron's a good name. I like it," she said. "I like you, too. I like the look of you, John Cameron. Are you down and out?"

"I've been down just now," he answered. He turned his head and looked steadfastly at the door of the saloon. "I'll be up again, though, perhaps."

"You want to go back in there and fight them? Don't be crazy. You come along with me," she commanded. "Dad needs a new man or two, and he'll give you a job. You come along with me."

She dismounted. She touched his arm, and his eyes drew away from the picture of vengeance that had been growing across his mind.

"Yes . . . I'll go a ways with you," he said. "You get on the horse again."

"I don't ride when a friend is walking," she answered. "Come along, John Cameron."

He walked beside her down the middle of the street. She was not very tall. Her forehead would touch his chin, just about. That, it appeared, was the right height. She was not heavy and she was not light, except in the quick grace of her movements. She had a voice that he must have heard before. He said that aloud: "Have I heard you speak before today?"

"I don't know. I'm pretty noisy. I do a lot of talking." She smiled. "Have you been around this town?"

"No," he answered. "But it seems as though I've heard your voice before. The sound of it strikes in a certain place and makes echoes. It makes me happy."

She slowed her step and looked up at him with a frown. "Are you saying that just for my benefit, because you think it sounds nicely?" she demanded.

"Are you angry?" asked Cameron. "I'm sorry."

"No, I guess you mean it, all right," she decided aloud. "But just for a minute I wondered . . . well . . . let it go. What are you doing in town, John Cameron?"

"I'm looking for a man . . . and I think I've found him," he said.

"Is that good news or bad news for him?" said the girl.

"I have to kill him," said Cameron slowly.

She looked suddenly up at him again.

"Shouldn't I have said that?" he asked her.

"Great Scott, John," she answered, "do you mean that you're out on a blood trail . . . you . . . at your age. . . ."

"I'm twenty-two," he said.

"And going to kill a man? Why, John?"

"Because he murdered my friend."

"Murdered? But there's the law. You can't. . . ."

He lifted his hands and looked down at them curiously. "If the law hanged him, there would be nothing that filled my hands . . . there would be no feeling . . . there would be no taste," said Cameron gently.

"Good heavens," said the girl. "You do mean it."

"You're angry. And that makes me unhappy."

"Not angry. But horrified. Really on a blood trail. Are you sure that your friend was murdered?"

"He was tied with wire and left in a burning cabin," said Cameron. "And I came back before he was dead."

They were beyond the edge of the town. The girl halted, looking straight up into Cameron's eyes, but he was staring beyond her at the vision from the past.

"He lived long enough to tell me what sort of horse the murderer rode. He told me that, and then he asked me for my gun. Then he killed himself."

"No!" cried the girl. "No, no, no. It isn't possible that you gave him the gun and let him kill himself."

"He was burned," said Cameron, "until his face was loose with cooking. It was ready to rub away. He was burned like a roast on a spit. That was why I gave him the gun. Before he had to begin screaming with pain. Ah . . . I'm sorry."

The girl, making an odd bubbling noise in the back of her throat, had slumped suddenly against the shoulder of the horse.

Chapter Three
Death Pledge

He could not tell what to do, but the sight of her helplessness made him feel strangely helpless also. He touched her with his hands and his eyes, reverently, and this reverence seemed to restore her strength. She was able to stand straight again. The mare turned her head inquisitively toward the mistress and was pushed away by a touch that was also a caress. The paths in the girl's mind had been cleared of everything else so that she could concentrate on Cameron's problem.

"*That* is what I saw in your face?" she demanded.

"What else could I do?" asked Cameron.

"I don't know. I only know it was terrible. I never heard of anything so terrible. It makes me want to help you. How can I help you, John?"

"By letting me come to you whenever you're in trouble . . . whenever you need any sort of help. By letting me walk up the road with you."

"Walk up the road?" she repeated, bewildered.

"This is the happiest thing I've ever done," he answered. "Walking up this road with you, I mean." At this, her eyes avoided him, and her color grew warmer. "That was a wrong thing to say. I've hurt you by saying that," he declared.

"No," she said. "It's not the wrong thing to say. John, I don't think you *could* say the wrong thing."

He felt his face grow hot. He swallowed, and said after a moment of silence: "I haven't seen very much of people, and I don't know how to talk." He walked on beside her. "But is this a happiness for you, too?"

"Yes."

"As though, when the road climbed that hill, we'd find something wonderful on the other side of it?"

She laughed. "A sort of road through the sky?" she asked.

"Exactly that! How did you happen to think of it? How did you know what I was thinking."

"I don't know. It's strange," she said.

She began to laugh, and he laughed with her, and their voices made together a music of two parts, high and deep, but with only one theme. He was aware of that. It delighted him, and it also delighted her. Their laughter stopped, and they looked at one another with shining eyes. But still they were walking on, and at this moment they passed the top of the hill beyond which, he had said, they might find that the road was laid through the sky. What they saw was a string of a dozen or more Indians, riding across the main trail, blanketed Indians who only lacked feathers in their hair to give them the exact look of the old days. They crossed into the trees and were gone.

"I knew we'd see *something* strange," said the girl. "They're heading up toward the new reservation."

Something had stirred Cameron's heart, and he looked earnestly after the vanished file of riders. But now a turn of the trail brought them to the Peyton ranch, suddenly, the confusion of the big corrals, a grove of cottonwoods, and the low, broad forehead of the house itself, showing over the rim of the rise.

Her father would be inside, she said. She gave her mare to a boy who loitered near the hitching rack and took Cameron straight into the house. He hung back.

"What's the matter?" she asked.

"My clothes are ragged. They're dusty and dirty."

"Your skin is clean, and so are your eyes. That's what counts. You come along in and don't be afraid of anything. Father needs a man like you on the place."

The living room was a big, barn-like place where a dance or a meeting could have been held. Over in a corner, in a leather chair, sprawled a man with gray hair and a grayish, care-worn face. He looked up from some papers spread out before him and rumbled: "Well, Jack, what have you brought home?"

"John Cameron," said the girl. "And he's a lot to bring. He wants a job, and you'll give him a place. You *need* him."

Peyton smiled a little. "You know how these dog-gone girls are, don't you?" he asked. "The newest dress and the newest man are the only things that count."

Cameron did not smile. He was too seriously and deeply examining the fatherly kindness of that face.

"I want men who can ride and shoot," said Peyton. "We have some rough horses, and some pretty handy gents in long loops have been helping themselves to the herds. They got one of our men just last week. Can you ride and shoot?"

Cameron laughed. With Mark Wayland he never had had horseflesh to ride unless it were wild-caught, fiercely savage, vengeful, cruel. "Yes, I can ride," he said. "I can shoot pretty well, too."

"Good with a rope?"

"I never had one in my hands," said Cameron. "But I can learn."

"Yeah," growled Peyton. "Boys can learn how to handle a rope. But only God can teach 'em to shoot fast and straight. Let me see how good you can shoot. Here, come over to this window. . . . Got a gun on you?"

"No."

"Take this," the rancher said, handing over his own gun, obviously too intent on the demonstration to wonder how Cameron had come to be without one. "Look yonder. You see the crow on top of that fence? Knock him off of it."

"It's not fair, Dad!" exclaimed the girl.

"Sure it ain't fair," said Peyton. "But there's nothing any closer for him to blaze away at."

He passed his gun to Cameron, and they saw him stand a little straighter, with his head raised in a peculiar pride and

119

eagerness. Many unfortunate men were to learn the meaning of that lifting of the head before the end of his trail. He gave to the target a single glance. His hand swept up, bearing the flash of the gun. The nose of it jerked as the weapon exploded. The crow leaped from the fence post and swung into the air.

"Missed," said Peyton.

"Try again!" cried the girl. "It was a close one."

"It will fall," said Cameron, calmly. "It is dying on the wing."

Peyton shrugged. "What makes you think you hit it? No feathers flew."

"I always know when the bullet strikes," said Cameron.

"What tells you?" scowled Peyton.

"I can't say. But I know."

Peyton glared at the girl, and she shrugged her shoulders as she answered the glance. This sort of calm egotism was not to her taste any more than it was to the taste of her father. But now Peyton exclaimed: "By thunder! Look."

The crow, flapping hard, circling for height, seemed to fall suddenly from the edge of his invisible tower in the sky. Down he came, blown into a ragged bundle of feathers by the wind, and struck the ground with a thump that was audible to the three watchers. Cameron gave the gun back to Peyton.

"How did you know you'd slugged that bird?" demanded Peyton, almost angrily.

"Well . . . I *feel* which way the bullet goes," said Cameron. "I've hunted a good deal when every bullet *had* to be turned into a dead rabbit or a deer. You learn to feel just where the bullet is going."

He made this speech with such a simplicity that all at once Peyton began to smile.

"All right, Cameron," he said. "I want you on this place. You're hired."

Hoofbeats swept up to the front of the house, paused. Almost at once there trampled into the room three big men. One of them was Will Tierney.

''There's a dance at Ripton,'' called out Tierney. ''Going with me, Jack?'' Then his voice changed as he barked out: ''What's the idea, bringing 'breeds home, Jack?''

''What do you mean?'' asked the girl. She cried it out and made a quick step away from Cameron.

'''Breed?'' growled her father. ''Have you got greaser in you, Cameron? By God, you have.''

Big Tierney and the other two men were striding closer. ''Throw him out,'' said Tierney. ''Think of the gall of him, coming out here. By God, think of it Jack, what's the matter with you? Can't you see the smoke in the eye?''

Cameron looked not at all at this approaching danger. He considered the girl only and saw her eyes widen with horror and disgust. She caught a hand to her breast as though she were struck to the heart by some memory. He knew what that memory was. It was their walk together up the road. It would stay in her mind, now, like dirt ingrained in the skin. It would be a foulness in her recollection.

Hands fell on him. But they could do nothing to him compared with the look in the great, stricken eyes of the girl as she turned away from him. Then Cameron turned toward the others. The two tall, fair-haired men had something of the look of Jacqueline about them. They were her brothers, perhaps.

''Kick him out!'' shouted one of them. ''We don't want no damned 'breeds here.''

''I'll leave the place and never come back,'' said Cameron. ''But if you handle me, I'll return and kill you, one by one, I swear to God.''

''D'you hear him, the dirty half-breed!'' cried Tierney, and he struck Cameron across the mouth with the flat of his hand. They swept Cameron to the window and hurled him through it. He landed on his head and shoulders, rolled over, and came staggering to his feet.

''If I have a look at you again,'' called Tierney, ''I'll take a whip to you myself!''

Chapter Four
Courage Call

In a wind-swept ravine among the hills the campfire blew aside, sharply slanting, fluttering the flames to blueness, making them shrink close to the sticks that were burning. The circle of blanketed figures around that fire was very dimly illumined. Young John Cameron, standing in the center of the circle, near the fire, could be seen more clearly. Instinct had made him select the leader of the party. He had to face the wind in order to look at the old man. He had to stiffen his lips and raise his voice against the blast. Sometimes he was almost shouting. And his breath was short as he came to the end.

"I have told you everything. The white men kick me out of their way like dirt. The white women loathe me. Therefore, I am not one of their people. If I am not a white man, then I am an Indian. Let me come with you."

There was a slight turning of heads as all looked toward the old man. He rose, tapped the ashes out of his pipe, and stepped close to Cameron. He was so very old the million wrinkles on his face were like knife cuts, but the eyes, folded back behind drooping lids, were as bright as youth itself.

He laid on the breast of Cameron the tip of a forefinger as hard as naked bone. "My son," he said, and the words blew with the wind and entered the mind of Cameron. "My son, when the heart is sick, men turn to new places. But they find no happiness except among their own kind. What is your kind? The white people will not have you. But you have an eye too open and wide. You are not an Indian. We cannot take you. You would bring new ways to us. You are neither white nor

Indian. You must live your own life in your own world. Or else you must fight the white men or the Indians until they take you in. All people are glad to have a man of whom they are afraid. Find the best man among many and ask him. He will tell you what to do.''

The wind was at Cameron's back, helping him, and it was still early night when he came again into the long, winding main street of the town of Gallop. Fire still burned in the forge of the blacksmith. He was still hammering at his anvil when the voice at his door made him look up and see the same agile, light form he had noticed that same morning.

"Will you name the best man in Gallop?" Cameron was asking.

"The *best* man?" The blacksmith laughed. "Les Harmody is the best man, all right."

"Where shall I find him?"

"He's in the old Tucker house, down the street. He moved in there the other day and unrolled his pack. Fourth house from the corner, in the middle of the big lot."

Cameron found the place easily. His mind was weighted by the sense of a double duty. He had to find Will Tierney and make sure that Tierney was indeed the murderer of Wayland. But when he killed Tierney, it must be not as a sneaking man-slayer but as a man of accepted name and race. Les Harmody might be the man to tell him what to do. He had heard the name before, but he could not tell how or where. Wayland himself must have spoken of Harmody. But the name had always been attached to something great. He was an old man, no doubt, and loaded with the wisdom of the years. So Cameron tapped with a reverent hand at the door of the shack. A faint light seeped through the cracks in the flimsy wall.

"Come in!" thundered a great voice.

He pulled the door open and stepped inside. The wind slammed the door shut behind him because what he saw loosened the strength of his fingers. He never had seen such a

123

man; he never had hoped to see one. Somewhere between youth and grayness—young enough to retain speed of hand and old enough to have his strength hardened upon him—Les Harmody filled the mind and the eye. He was not a giant in measured inches or in counted pounds, but he struck the imagination with a gigantic force. He was magnificent rather than handsome. The shaggy forelock and the weight of the jaw gave a certain brutality to his face, but the enormous power that clothed his shoulders and his arms was the main thing. His wrist was as round and as hard as an apple, filled with compacted sinews of power and the iron bone of strength underneath. He was eating a thick steak with a mug of coffee placed beside it. Gristle or bone in the last mouthful crackled between his teeth now.

"Are you Les Harmody?" asked Cameron.

The other nodded.

"I've come to ask you a question," said Cameron. He stepped closer to the table.

"You're Wayland's 'breed, ain't you?" asked the great voice.

Cameron stopped, stiffening suddenly.

"I don't talk to 'breeds. I don't have them in the same place with me. Get out," commanded Harmody.

"I go without talking? Like a dog?"

"All 'breeds is dogs."

"Dogs have teeth," answered Cameron, and, stepping still closer, he leaned and flicked his hand across the face of the giant.

Harmody rose without haste. His eye measured several things: Cameron and the distance to the door that assured him the victim could not escape. He leaned one great hand on the table and in the other raised the mug of coffee, which he emptied at a draught. He wiped his dripping lips on the back of his hand as he put down the cup.

"I've come to ask a question, and I'll have your answer,"

said Cameron. "I'll have it . . . if I have to tear it out of your throat."

Harmody did not walk around the table. He brushed it aside with a light gesture, and all the dishes on it made a clattering.

"You'll tear it out of me?" he said softly, and then he lunged for Cameron.

Up there in the mountain camps, patiently, with fists bare, Mark Wayland had taught his foster son something of the white man's art of self-defense. Cameron used the lessons now. He had no hope of winning; he only hoped that he might prove himself a man. Speed of foot shifted him aside from the first rush. He hit Harmody three times on the side of the jaw as the big target rushed past. It was like hitting a great timber with sacking wrapped over it.

Harmody stopped his rush, turned. He pulled a gun and tossed it aside. "I'm gonna kill you," he said through his teeth, "but I don't want tools to do the job. A greasy 'breed . . . a damned, greasy 'breed . . . to make a fool out of me, eh?"

He came again, not blindly, but head up, balanced, inside himself, as a man who understands boxing advances. Even if he had been totally ignorant, to stand to him would have been like standing to a grizzly. But he had skill to back up his power. He was fast, bewilderingly fast for a man of his poundage. He feinted with a left. He repeated with the same hand, and the blow grazed Cameron's head. It was as though the hoof of a brass-shod stallion had glanced from his skull. The weight of the blow flung him back against the wall, and Harmody rushed in to grasp a helpless victim.

His arms reached for nothingness. Cameron had slid away with a ducking side-step. He had to look on his own fists as tack hammers. They would only avail if they hit the right place a thousand times, breaking down some nerve center with repeated shocks. The swift blows thudded on Harmody's jaw, as he swayed around. He tried the left feint and, again, the blow was side-stepped.

Wings were under Cameron's feet, and he felt and used them. If only there were more room than this shack afforded— if only he had space to maneuver in, then he could swoop and retreat and swoop again until he had beaten this monster into submission. But he had to keep a constant thought of the walls, the overturned chairs, the table which had crashed over on its side and extended its legs to trip him. And one slip, one fall, would be the end of him. Those dreadful hands of Harmody would break him in an instant, but every moment he was growing more sure, more steady. He changed from the jaw and shot both hands for the wind. His right thumped on the ribs as on the huge round of a barrel; but the left dug deep into the rubbery stomach muscles, and Harmody grunted. A second target, that made. And then he reached Harmody's glaring eyes with hooking punches that jarred back the massive head. He reached the wide mouth and puffed and cut the lips. They fought silently, except for the noise of their gasping breath. Always there was the terrible danger that one of Harmody's blows would get fairly home. Then the devil that was lodged behind his eyes would have its chance at full expression. A glancing blow laid open Cameron's cheek. He felt the hot running of the blood down his face.

But that was nothing. Nothing compared with the stake for which he fought. Not merely to endure for a time, but actually to win, to conquer, to beat this great hulk into submission. He fought for that. He never struck in vain—for the eyes, for the mouth, for the vulnerable side of the chin, or for the soft of the belly—those were his targets. A hammer stroke brushed across his own mouth—merely brushed across it—but slashed the lips open and brought a fresh downpour of blood. In return, he stepped aside and tattooed the body and then the jaw of Harmody.

The big fellow was no longer an exhaustless well of energy, but now he paused between rushes. His mouth opened wide to take greater breath. Sweat dripped down his face and mingled with the blood. But the flaming devil in his eyes was still bright.

Exhaustion began to work in Cameron, also. He had to run, to dance, to keep himself poised as on wings. And the preliminary tremors of weakness began to run through his body constantly. He saw that the thing would have to come to a crisis. He would have to bring it to an end—meet one of those headlong charges and literally knock the monster away from him. It was impossible—but it was the only way. He saw the rush start, and he moved as though to leap to either side. Instead, he sprang in, ducked the driving fist that tried to catch him, and hammered a long overhand right straight against Harmody's jaw.

The solid shock, his running weight and lashing blow against Harmody's rush, turned his arm numb to the shoulder. But Harmody was stopped. He was halted, he was put back on his heels; he was making little short steps to the rear, to regain his balance. Cameron followed like a greedy wildcat. The right hand had no wits in it, now. He used the left, then, and with three full drives he found Harmody's chin. He saw the great knees buckle. The head and shoulders swayed. The guarding, massive arms dropped first, and then Les Harmody sank to the floor. Cameron stepped back. He wanted to run in and crash his fist home behind the ear—a stroke that would end the fight even if Harmody were a giant. But there were rules in this game, and a fallen man must not be hit. So Cameron stood back, groaning with eagerness, and saw the loosened hulk on its knees and on one supporting hand.

"Have you got enough" gasped Cameron.

"Me?" groaned Les Harmody. "Me? Enough? Damn your rotten heart. . . ."

He lurched to his feet. Indignation seemed to burn the darkness out of his brain, and again he was coming in. Once more Cameron stepped in to check the rush. This time his fist flew high—his right shoulder was still aching from the first knockdown—and he felt the soggy impact against the enormous, blackened cushion which covered the spot where the eyes of Harmody should have been shining. It was a hard blow, but it was not enough to stop Harmody. Before Cameron's eyes loomed a great fist. He tried to jerk his head away from its path, but it jerked upward too swiftly. The shock seemed not under the jaw but at the back of his head. He fell forward on his face. . . .

Consciousness came back to him, after that, in lurid flashes. He had a vague knowledge that told him he would be killed, certainly. He was dead already. It was his ghost that was wakening in another world. Then he was aware of lights around him, and the wide flash of a mirror's face. There were exclaiming voices. There was a greater voice than all others, the thunder of Les Harmody. A mighty hand upheld him, wavering. A powerful shoulder braced against him.

He looked, now, and saw his own face, dripping crimson, swollen, purple here and running blood there. He saw the face of Les Harmody beside his own—and the big man's features had been battered out of shape. On the left side there were no features. There was only a ghastly swollen mass of bruised, hammered flesh.

This monster was shouting, out of a lop-sided mouth: "Here's the fellow that stood up to me . . . me . . . Les Harmody! By God, I thought that the time would never come when I'd have the pleasure of standin' hand to hand with any one man. Look at him, you coyotes, you sneakin' house dogs that run and yammer like hell when a wolf comes to town! Look at him. Here's plenty of wolf for you. Look at the skinny size of him that fought Les Harmody, man to man, and knocked me down. And then, by God, he stood back and give me my chance to stand once more. I tell you, look at him, will you?"

The big bandanna of Harmody dipped into a schooner of beer. He drew it out, sopping, crushed the excess liquid out, and then carefully sponged the bleeding face of Cameron. The cold and the sting of the beer helped to rouse him completely.

"Speak up, one of you. D'you see him?" thundered Harmody. There was a murmur. "Grady, you fat-faced buzzard, d'you see him now? Is he a white man?"

"He's anything that you want to call him, Les."

"I ask you, is he white, damn you?"

"Sure. He's white, Les."

"The rat that ever calls him a 'breed again is gonna have me to reckon with afterwards. No, he don't need no help. He can go by himself. But, by God, he'll have fair play, man to man. Listen, kid . . . are you feelin' better? I wanted them to see you, and what you done to me. I wanted the whole damn' world to see. Kid, will you drink with me? Can you stand, and can you drink? Whiskey, Grady. Damn you, move fast. Whiskey for the kid. Here, feller, I've been searching the world for a gent with the nerve and the hands to stand up to me. Here's to the man that done it. Every one of you *hombres* liquor up on this. Take a look at him. He's a man. He's a M-A-N! Drink to him. Bottoms up."

This was the beginning of John Cameron's friendship with Les Harmody. In the weeks that followed, Harmody worked with the younger man in breaking horses. Cameron, at Harmody's urging, even successfully entered the bronc' riding event at the annual rodeo in Ripton, and afterward Harmody presented Cameron with a pair of golden spurs as a gift. It was Harmody's way of showing the world at large that he believed John Cameron to be the equal of any man. Jacqueline Peyton was among the spectators at the rodeo. She had come to regret deeply the way she had behaved when Cameron had been thrown off her father's ranch, but she hesitated to speak to him of what was in her heart. Her engagement to Will Tierney had been recently announced by her father, and she did not wish to be the cause of further trouble between the two men.

Chapter Five
'Breed Law

One night about a month after the Ripton rodeo there was music in the Peyton house. Joe Peyton thrummed a banjo. Harry Peyton and Will Tierney sang. Jacqueline was at the piano, and her father, Oliver Peyton, composed himself in a deep chair with his hands folded behind his head, a contented audience. They had not heard the pounding hoofs of a big horse approach the house, but they were aware of the creaking of the floor in the hall as someone walked toward them, and now the great figure that loomed in the doorway silenced the song in the middle. Oliver Peyton jumped to his feet.

"Hey, Les Harmody," he called. "I'm glad to see you, old son. Come in and sit down. You know everybody. What you drinking?"

Harmody accepted the extended hand rather gingerly. "Thanks, Ollie," he said. "I'm not drinking. And for what I've got to say, I reckon that standing will be the best. Sorry to break in on you folks like this. Hello, Jacqueline. Hello, Will. Hello, everybody. Glad to see you . . . and sorry to see you, too."

"What's the matter, Les?" urged Oliver Peyton, frowning anxiously. "You talk as though you had a grudge, old-timer?"

"By a way of speaking I ain't got a grudge," said Harmody. "But in another way, I got a pretty deep one. I've come from a friend, and a better friend no man ever had. You know John Cameron?"

"The 'breed?" asked Tierney.

Harmody started. "That's the wrong word for him, Will.

130

I've stood up and told people that 'breed ain't the word for him. But maybe you weren't around when I did my talking. His grandmother was a Blackfoot girl that could've married a chief and done him proud. His father and all his line are as white as white. Understand?''

''Blood is blood,'' said Tierney calmly. ''He's just a 'breed to me.''

Harmody took in a big breath. ''We'll find a better place to argue it out, one day.''

''Any place and any time would be good for me,'' said Tierney, and his bright eyes measured Harmody steadily.

''Quit it, Will!'' commanded Oliver Peyton. ''It only riles up Les. Can't you see that? Les, I wish you'd sit down.''

''I'll say it standing,'' answered Harmody. ''I've been away in the hills for pretty near a month now with Cameron. It takes time to learn to know a friend, but I've learned to know him. On a horse or on his feet, with his hands or with a gun, I never found a better man. But he's got ideas.'' He paused, after he said this, and ran his eyes over the group, his glance dwelling for a moment on the face of the girl. She had grown pale. ''Jacqueline,'' said Harmody, ''maybe you know what news I've got?''

''I can guess it,'' she answered.

Her father stared at her.

''I've done a lot of talking and reasoning with him,'' went on Harmody, ''but the main thing is that he feels he's given his word, and he's given it to God Almighty. So he'll keep it. Right here in this room he gave his promise.''

''He did,'' said the girl through colorless lips.

''What promise?'' asked Oliver Peyton.

''When Will and Joe and Harry had their hands on him, he told them that if they threw him out, he'd kill them. He swore to God that he would.''

''What kind of damned rot is this?'' demanded Oliver Peyton. ''I heard that, too . . . but it's rot.''

''Why, he's a crazy fool,'' declared young Joe Peyton.

"Harmody," said Oliver Peyton, "you mean to say that fellow . . . that man, Cameron . . . that he's going to come on the trail of my boys?"

"He gave 'em a fair warning," said Harmody. "There was three of them, and he gave them a fair warning not to handle him. And then they done it. I tell you, Ollie, a promise is a mighty sacred thing to that Cameron."

"There's a law," said the rancher, "and I'll have the sheriff and his men out."

"Hell, Oliver," said Harmody, "you might as well ask the sheriff and his boys to try and catch a wild hawk. I'm telling you the truth. They'll never see hide nor hair of him."

"You mean that the young snake is down here now?" shouted Peyton.

"He ain't near," replied Harmody. "The fact is that he's the kind that never hits below the belt. I've talked and argued with him. I've begged him to think it over, because a killing is most usually murder in the eyes of the law. But he can't get it out of his head that he's made a promise to God Almighty to kill the three of 'em. Arguin' won't budge him." Then he added: "But he wants you all to be warned fair and square that he's coming after you. You'll kill him, or he'll kill you."

This struck a silence across the room.

Harmody went on: "You're the special one, Tierney, and he mostly wants to have the killing of you, because he says that you sure killed his partner over at their mine."

"He's a madman," said Tierney. "Accusing *me* of murder, eh? All that a mad dog can see is red."

"He says that there was around fifty pounds in gold dust. And he points out that inside the last ten days you've made a payment on the land where you're going to live with Jacqueline, yonder. You've made that payment. . . ."

"I don't follow all this!" exclaimed Tierney loudly.

But Harmody said: "You can't drown me out till I've made

my point. You made that payment with thirty pounds of the same sort of gold dust.''

"Will!" cried the girl.

"You damned sneaking blackguard!" shouted Tierney. He strode at Harmody, but Oliver Peyton stepped between and stopped the younger man.

"I know that you're a mighty brave and bright young man, Will," said Peyton, "but don't you start anything with Les Harmody. He's just too old and tough to be chawed up by youngsters."

Harmody backed up to the door. "I come in here being sorry that I had to bring bad news," he said. "But the longer I've stayed here, the more I've felt that the kid is right. There's something damned rotten in the air. Tierney, I think the kid is right about *you* . . . and if you done that job, God help your soul."

He was gone through the doorway at once.

Behind him Tierney was saying: "Something has to be done about this. A skunk like that 'breed going about the county, poisoning the air with his lies. . . ."

"Will," said the girl, "*is* it a lie?"

He spun about on his heel and confronted her and her white face. "Jack, are you *believing* him?" he shouted.

She stared at him for a moment. "I don't know," she said. "I don't know what to believe, except that John Cameron is an honest man."

She saw everything clearly. It would be a battle of three against one, and poor John Cameron must die unless Harmody threw in with him. Even so, that meant a battle. There was only one way to stop the fighting. That was to induce Cameron to leave the country. And if she could find the way to him. . . .

This thought got her out of the room at once. In the corral she caught up her favorite mare and was quickly on the road. Far away—north on the trail or south on the trail, east or west on it, or more likely wandering straight across country—big Les Harmody was traveling now. She turned in the saddle with a desperate eagerness, scanning the horizon, and so made out, very dimly, the movement of a shape over a hill and against the horizon. She struck out in that direction at once. It was the eastern trail, and she flew the mare along it for half a mile. After that she slowed to a walk and heard distinctly, out of the distance, the clacking of hoofs over a stretch of stony ground. She would have to go very carefully; she would have to hunt like an Indian if she wished to trail this man and remain unheard.

As she came up the next rise, it seemed to her that she heard other hoofbeats behind her, but that was, no doubt, a sheer mental illusion, or a trick of echoes. Before her in the night there was no longer sound or sight of the big horseman. She pressed on at a gallop, giving up all hope of secrecy in her pursuit.

"Les," she began to cry aloud. "Les Harmody!"

A deep-throated shout answered her at once. She saw the huge man and the huge horse looming against the stars above the next hummock.

"That you, Jacqueline?" asked Harmody, as she came up. "What's wrong?"

"Nothing much," she answered. "Cameron is after my two brothers. He'll probably kill them, or they'll kill him, and that won't make me any richer."

"What do you want to do?" he asked.

"I want to beg John to leave the country."

"It's no use," said Harmody. "He won't go."

"I want to try, though. I have to try to persuade him."

"D'you like Cameron?"

"I like him a lot."

"Come along, then. A woman can always do what a man can't manage. I've begged him hard to give up this job. He's been like a stone, though."

They rode on together, leaving the trail presently and plunging into a thicket of brush higher than their heads. Finally, through the dark mist of brush, she could see the pale gleam of a light that showed them a small clearing where the ruins of a squatter's shack leaned feebly to the side, ready to fall. By the fire Cameron answered the call of Harmody.

"Who's coming with you?" he snapped. "What made you . . . ?" He broke off when he saw the girl. He had been thinner the last time he had talked to her, and he looked older now even than he had at the Ripton rodeo. Across one cheekbone was the jagged red of a scar that time, perhaps, would gradually dim. He wore better clothes. Perhaps they helped him to a new dignity. She went straight up to him, after she had dismounted, and offered her hand.

"I insulted you once, by keeping silent when I should have spoken up," she said. "Can you forgive that, John?"

He took her hand, with a touch softer than that of a woman. His grave eyes studied her face. "They told you the truth," he said. "I am a half-breed."

"It isn't the blood. It's the man that counts," she answered. "And I'm beginning to realize what a man you are. I guessed it when we walked up that road together. I knew it when I heard what you'd done to Les Harmody and saw you ride at Ripton. It's because I know what a man you are that I've come here tonight."

"Les should never have brought you," he said.

"She follered me, John," protested Harmody. "Don't be hard on me about that. What was I to do? Besides, I thought that she might show you the best way out of this whole mess."

"That's it, of course," said Cameron gloomily. "I have to be persuaded. But there's no good in that, Jacqueline. There's no good at all. I've given a promise that I'll have to keep."

She was silent.

"You see how it is?" said the grumbling voice of Harmody. "Nothing can budge him."

"There's only one thing I wish," said Cameron, "that none of them meant anything to you."

"Why do you wish that?" she asked him.

"You remember when we walked up the road together?"

135

"I'll never forget that."

"If I could keep you from sorrow, I'd like to. You know, Jacqueline, now that I see you here and remember that some of your look is in your brothers, I don't think that I could harm them. But Tierney . . . I know you're going to marry him . . . Tierney has to be rubbed off my books."

"He's nothing to me," said the girl.

"He has to be. You're marrying him!" protested Cameron.

"I give you my word and my honor, he's nothing to me tonight. Because I think . . . I *really* believe . . . that he did the frightful thing you've accused him of."

"You're through with him?"

"Yes."

"I don't believe that," said Cameron sternly. "If you love a man, you'll never give him up, even if he has a thousand murders on his back."

"It was never love. It was simply growing up together, and going riding and dancing together, and being encouraged by everyone."

"Ah?" said Cameron. "Would a woman marry a man for no better reasons than that?"

She felt the scorn and the horror in his voice. She flushed. "I'm afraid women do," she answered. "John, have you become so hard, so stern? Is there no use, my trying to talk to you?"

"I can listen to you better than I can listen to running water in the desert. Sit down here, Jacqueline. Here, by the fire. That's better. I can see your eyes now, you know. Whenever they stir, my heart stirs. When you look up at me like this, my heart leaps like a fish."

"Hey," said Les Harmody, "you can't talk to a girl like that."

"Can't I?" asked Cameron, startled. "Have I said something wrong?"

"Not a word," said the girl.

"Help me to teach him something," said Harmody. "All

he knows is hunting and reading. He don't know nothing about people. You can't let a gent talk to you like that."

"Why not? I like it," she said.

"But dog-gone it, Jacqueline, unless he loves you, or something like that. . . ."

"I do," said Cameron. "Does that make it all right?"

"Hey, wait! Wait!" shouted big Les Harmody. "What's the matter with you? You've only met her once before."

"It's true," said Cameron. "But that was more happiness in a few minutes than all the rest of my life put together."

"Well, then, you gotta learn not to say everything you think right out loud to a girl. They ain't used to it. You gotta spend a lot of time approaching a woman. You gotta be more dog-gone particular than when you come up on the blind side of a horse. Ain't I right, Jacqueline?"

"Not about John," she answered.

"Hold on. What's his special edge on the rest of us?"

"I don't know," said the girl. "But I like everything he says."

"Hold on, Jacqueline!" shouted Harmody. "Hold on, there. If you get ideas into his head, you'll never get them out again."

"I don't want to get them out again," she answered.

"Don't say that. I mean," explained Harmody, "that if you give him half a chance, he'll start ragin' like a dog-gone forest fire."

The girl smiled up at Harmody. "You know a lot about girls, Les," she said, "but John Cameron happens to know a lot about me." She put out a hand and touched Cameron's arm. "That's why I've had the courage to come up here to-night," she said. "It *couldn't* go on, John, you couldn't take a blood trail behind my brothers."

"No," said Cameron breathlessly, leaning toward her. "I couldn't lay a finger on them."

"And Tierney . . . leave him to the law. There is a law for that sort of a man."

"I can't leave him. I told you that before. If you were I . . . if you'd been raised by Wayland and then found him dying, as I found him, wouldn't you despise yourself if you waited for the law to do your work on the murderer?"

She held her breath, fighting back the answer that rose into her throat, but it burst out in spite of her.

"Yes, I would!" she exclaimed. "I don't blame you a bit."

"Quit talking that way," commanded Harmody. "D'you know that you'll have him out raisin' hell right away, if you talk to him like that?"

"I'm only begging one thing," said the girl. "You've held your hand all this time. Will you wait another month before you take that trail? Will you let the law see what it can do, first of all?"

He dropped his face between his hands and stared at the fire. Les Harmody, making vast, vague signs of encouragement from the background, edged off to a little distance. The girl looked up at the giant with a flashing smile of confidence.

John Cameron raised his head to answer, the trouble gradually clearing away from his eyes, when the voice of Tierney barked from the edge of the brush: "Stick up those hands! Fast!"

"What in hell?" began Harmody.

"You're out of this, Les!" shouted the voice of Joe Peyton.

Cameron had risen to his feet. The girl threw herself in front of him.

"Joe, don't shoot!" she screamed. "Will, don't shoot at him! The poor fellow didn't mean anything . . . he only has half a brain, Will."

Chapter Six
The Death Trap

Will Tierney came out from the brush at a strange, gliding pace, his feet touching the earth softly in concern that nothing might upset his aim, his revolver held well out before his body.

"Get away from him, Jack!" he shouted. "Step away, or I'll drill him through you, by God."

Cameron had waited a single second, stunned. His gun belt and gun had been laid aside. His hands were empty, and death was stalking him. But what really mattered was that the girl had called him a half-wit. Had she come merely for the purpose of holding him and Les Harmody helpless while her fighting men came up to wipe out the 'breed? He thought of that. Then he turned and dived for the brush. He ran as a snipe flies, dodging rapidly from side to side and yelling: "Harmody, it's my fight. Stay out of it!"

He heard the scream of the girl, then the guns began to boom. Bullets whistled past his head, right and left, and then the sudden thunder of Les Harmody's voice broke in. The gunfire continued. But the bullets no longer whirred past him. The brush crashed before his face. He was instantly in the thick gloom of the foliage, safe for that moment, and he heard the shrill cry of the girl: "Will! You've killed Les Harmody!"

That voice struck him to a halt. He stood, gripping at the trunk of a young sapling until the palm of his hand ached, and behind him he heard Harmody's deep, broken voice exclaiming: "I'm all right, Jacqueline. Don't worry about me. I'm all right. But I tell the rest of you for your own good . . . don't go into that brush after Cameron. If you go in there, he'll kill

139

you as sure as God made wildcats. Keep out of the darkness
. . . he ain't got a gun. But he's got hands that are almost as
good as a gun.''

They did not press into the brush, but Will Tierney yelled:
''Here's hell to pay! It's the 'breed that ought to be lying here,
not Harmody. Les, it's your own fault. If you hadn't got in
between me and my aim, I'd have Cameron dead as a bone.
He dodged . . . damn him, he dodged like a bird in the air. I
never saw such a rabbit.''

''You never saw such a man-eater, either,'' declared Harmody. ''And he'll chaw your bones one day, Mister Murderer
Tierney.''

''Murderer?'' shouted Tierney. ''You mean to say that you
believe his yarn about me?''

''Stop talking, Les,'' commanded the girl. ''Save your
breath. Help me carry him into the shack. Joe . . . Harry, take
his shoulders. Does that hurt you, Les? Gently, boys.''

Back to the edge of the clearing ventured Cameron and from
the thick of the brush watched the men carrying huge Les
Harmody through the open door of the shack. Will Tierney,
coming back into the clearing, kicked some more fuel onto
the fire and made the flames jump. This brighter light seemed
to be a comfort to him. He walked in an uneasy circle around
the fire, staring toward the brush constantly.

In the meantime the conference inside the cabin could be
heard clearly. As it progressed, they were examining the
wound of Harmody. Once he groaned aloud as though under
a searching probe. Then the girl was saying: ''He ought to
have a doctor. I'll stay here with him. But he ought to have a
doctor by morning. The three of you go straight for town.''

''I'll stay here with you, Jack,'' said Harry Peyton.

''You'll do nothing of the kind,'' she answered. ''What if
John Cameron knew that there was only one man here?''

''He hasn't a gun,'' said Harry Peyton.

''He has his wits and his hands, and that's enough,'' said

big Les Harmody. "Jacqueline is dead right. The three of you stay close together all the time."

Tierney stepped to the door of the shack. "*Bah!*" he snarled. "I'd like nothing better than to tackle him alone. I'd love it."

"I think you like murder better'n you would ever like fighting," said Les Harmody.

"When you're on your feet," answered Tierney, "I'll give you your chance at me, any time."

"Thanks," said Harmody. "I'll take you up on that, one day."

"Be still," commanded the girl. "The three of you start riding . . . and start now. Keep bunched. Head for Gallop and get Doc Travis. We don't have to worry about Les for a while. Those big ribs of his turned the bullet a bit. And it's better to have broken ribs than a bullet through the heart. Will . . . you fired to kill."

"The fool came in my path," said Tierney. "What else was I to do? He came between me and Cameron."

"Who gave you the right to murder John Cameron?" she demanded.

"You talk as though I were a butcher, Jack."

"I think you are," she answered.

Strange joy rushed through Cameron's brain as he listened.

"Jack," cried Tierney, "does it mean that you're through with me?"

"I never want to see your face again," she replied.

Tierney strode into the shack, shouting something that was lost to the straining ears of Cameron because all the men were speaking at once. Then, through a pause, Cameron could hear Tierney snapping out: "You prefer a 'breed, maybe?"

"I prefer John Cameron . . . I don't care what you call him," she answered.

Not care? Not care even when he was called a 'breed? Did she, in truth, prefer John Cameron? He, lingering on the trembling verge of the firelight, the shadows wavering across his eyes, felt a weakness in the knees, a vague and uncertain awe.

The brothers were protesting. Harry Peyton was thundering: "Jack, you don't mean it. You can't mean it. A dirty half-breed? I'd rather see you. . . ."

"Shut your mouth, Harry," said the profound voice of Les Harmody. "Don't you speak to her like that."

The three men came striding out of the shack a moment later. "It's no good," Tierney was saying. "You can see that she's hypnotized by that rat of a Cameron. Joe, I'm going to have the killing of him."

"Not if I can get to him with a gun first," answered Joe.

They went away across the clearing hastily, and, as the brush closed after them, cracking behind their backs, there was a great impulse in Cameron to run forward to the shack and show himself for one instant to the girl he loved and to Les Harmody, who with his own body had stopped the bullets that were intended for his friend. Some rich day would come when he would have a chance to show Harmody that he was ready to die for him. He could understand, too, why the girl had called him a half-wit. It had been her first gesture toward stopping the attack of big Will Tierney, to assure him that his rival was a creature of no importance. But there was something more for Cameron to do than to speak to the woman he loved or to touch the hand of his friend. He had to strike Tierney. If God would let him, he had to strike at Tierney now, and he was on foot, he was weaponless, and there were three men against him, two of whom were sacred from any serious injury at his hands.

As the idea dawned in Cameron's mind, it seemed at first totally absurd. But he knew that Tierney would probably get out of the country as fast as possible. Tierney had lost his chance at the rich marriage. There now hung over his head the accusation of murder, and there was nothing to hold him in this part of the world except, perhaps, a desire to wipe out Cameron. But the great chances were that Tierney would ride with the Peytons, go as far as Gallop, deliver the message to the doctor, and then slip away toward an unknown destination.

There was no time to catch him, therefore, except on this night. And already the horses of the three were galloping steadily away. They would turn down through the hills and take the long, straight road offered by Lucky Chance Ravine, which pointed straight on at the town of Gallop. It was his consciousness of the probable course they would follow that taught Cameron what he could do. The riders would have to wind down through the hills to come to the head of the steep-walled ravine. For his own part, he could strike straight across and climb the walls wherever he chose. As he ran, he made his hands work. He snatched off his shirt, tore it into strips, and began to knot the tough strings together. He could have laughed to think that this was his weapon against three mounted, armed men.

Meantime he had been running as few people can. He had left the woods, slipped through a pass between two hills, and so found himself on the rim of Lucky Chance Ravine. It ran straight east toward Gallop, bordered with cliffs to the north and south, sheer faces of rock. It was not hard to get down the cliff face. On the level floor of the ravine, Cameron dodged among the rocks until he came to a narrows where the only clear passage was a ten-foot gap between two very large rocks. This was the strategic point for him. It was the thought of this gap through which the riders must pass in single file that had started him for Lucky Chance Ravine. Now he heard the distant clattering of hoofs that moved toward him with the steady lope which western horses understand, that effortless, pausing swing of the body, slower than any other gallop. He had very little time for his preparations, but his plan was simple enough.

He knotted one end of his clumsy rope around a ragged projection on the side of one boulder, then he crouched beside the other great rock with the loose end in his grip. The slack of the twisted rope lay flat on the ground. He had hardly taken his place before he saw them coming. He was crouched so low that he could see the heads and shoulders of the two in the lead against the stars, so that they seemed to be sweeping through the sky. Well behind them came the third party. He prayed that the last rider might be big Will Tierney.

He gauged his moment with the most precise care, then jerked up the rope, and laid his weight against it. Well below the knees of the horse the rope struck. There was a jerk that hurled Cameron head over heels, but, while he rolled, he saw horse and rider topple. As he scrambled to his feet, the mustang was beginning to rise, snorting, and the rider lay prone and still at a little distance. Cameron caught the reins of the mustang and led it to the fallen rider. He had to lean close to make out the features of the man in the dull starlight, and with a groan he recognized Joe Peyton. He thrust his hand inside Peyton's shirt and pressed it above the heart until he felt the reassuring pulsation. Not dead, but badly knocked out.

He got Joe Peyton's gun and flung himself on the back of the horse. It was at full gallop in a moment, speeding after the distant beat of hoofs. He rushed the horse, pressing its flanks with his spurs, and so the leading pair of riders came back to him through the night, growing visible, then larger and larger.

"All right, Joe?" shouted Harry Peyton.

He uttered a wordless whoop for answer, and the leaders sped on, unsuspicious. He could distinguish them one from the other now. Will Tierney was in the lead. Harry Peyton was two or three lengths behind Tierney. Therefore it was beside him that Cameron rushed his mustang, bringing the horse up so fast that Peyton had only time to twist in the saddle and cry out once in astonishment—for he could see, now, the gleam of the bare skin of Cameron. His cry was cut short. A clip across the head struck with the long barrel of Cameron's revolver dropped Peyton out of his saddle. Cameron, catching the loosened reins of the other horse, jerked the mustang to a halt. At the same time the yell of Will Tierney flashed across his brain.

Men said that Will Tierney feared nothing human. He must

have thought, then, that half-naked Cameron was a devil and not a man, for he dropped himself low over his saddle bow, gave his horse the spur, and raced it toward the distant lights of Gallop. Cameron had a strange feeling that luck was with him, that, having helped him past the first two stages of his night's work, it would not fail him in the last, important moment. But he found that Tierney was drawing away from him. Big Will Tierney, twisting in the saddle, tried three shots in rapid succession, and missed his mark. But to Cameron there would be no proper revenge in merely shooting a fugitive through the back. That would not repay him for the death of his friend. So he held his fire, and rode harder than before.

In another moment he had his reward. The far finer horse of Tierney had opened up a gap in the beginning, but the much greater weight of Tierney made up the difference after the first burst of speed. His mount began to flag, while the tough mustang that labored between the knees of Cameron gained steadily. Tierney dodged his horse through a nest of boulders. The mustang followed like a true cutting horse on the tail of a calf. Cameron was not a length behind when Tierney turned and fired again. And the mustang went down like a house of cards. The earth rose. Cameron's head struck fire through his brain. He fell into a thick darkness and lay still.

When he roused, at last, he was dripping with water. Another quantity of it had been sloshed over him by the figure that stood tall and black against the stars. A groan had passed involuntarily through the lips of Cameron.

"Coming to, kid?" asked Tierney's voice cheerfully. "I thought you'd never come around. Feeling better?"

Cameron tried to move, but found that his legs and hands had been bound together with something harder and colder than twine. Then he realized that he had been bound with wire—hard bound, so that the iron ground the flesh against the bones of his wrist and his ankle. He stared up at the stars and found them whirling into fire. Nearby, there was the sound of swiftly whispering water. And gradually he realized what had happened, and the sort of a death that he was likely to die.

Chapter Seven
A Dead Man's Lesson

"I'm to go the way that Mark Wayland went, eh?" asked Cameron.

Tierney had been carrying the revivifying water from the creek in Cameron's hat. Now he swished the hat idly back and forth, the final drops whipping into Cameron's face.

"Sure you're going the way of Mark Wayland. But to hell with him. Think about yourself."

"Wayland," said Cameron, as the confession came from Tierney, "never did harm to anyone. Why did you murder him?"

"Want to know what he did to me?"

"Nothing wrong," declared Cameron.

"If you say that again, I'll kick your face in. Listen . . . five years ago, when I was feeling pretty good, I got into a fight with a greaser fool . . . I never had any use for 'breeds and greasers."

"I know," agreed Cameron.

He was trying to think. Mark Wayland had always said that a good brain could cut a man's way through any difficulty. What device could he find to free himself from the danger of death now? At least, he might keep Tierney talking for a little time. Every moment saved was a chance gained, in that sense.

"This greaser," said Tierney," got me down on the floor of the barroom, and I pulled out a gun and let him have some daylight through his belly. He kicked himself around in circles and took a long time to die. You never heard anything like his screaming. I hung around and listened to the last of it, and

147

that was where I was a fool. There were half a dozen people around, but they felt the way I did . . . that killing a greaser was always self-defense. Then another man came . . . Mark Wayland. He heard what had happened and started for me. I pulled the gun on him, but he was a little faster.'' Tierney rubbed his right arm. ''Clipped me through the arm so that my gun dropped, and then he turned me over to the sheriff. The sheriff didn't want to pinch me, but after Wayland had done the pinching, the law started working. Nothing but murder. And me headed straight for the rope. But I managed to work my way out of the jail one night. That's one of the good things about this country . . . their cheesecloth jails.''

He recommenced on the theme of Wayland. ''You were saying that Wayland never did anybody harm. If I'd hanged, that would have been harm, wouldn't it? And living these years, never knowing when somebody might turn up and recognize me . . . that wasn't harm, eh?''

''Did Wayland recognize you?'' asked Cameron.

''I had a mask over my mug. I lay up there behind the rocks and watched you start out hunting. Then I slipped down to the shack and whanged him over the head. It was easy. I wired him up and touched a match to his clothes to wake him up. He wakened with a holler, too, like the sort of a noise that the greaser made on the barroom floor.''

It was strange and at the same time a horrible thing to look straight into the mind of a man without the slightest sense of right and wrong.

''He wasn't yelling at the end,'' remarked Cameron.

''No, he'd shut up as soon as he realized. Too much brute in him. Like an Indian. Pride and all that.''

Big Will Tierney sat down on a convenient rock and lit a cigarette. ''I thought that he'd break down,'' he said, ''when I pointed out what I was going to do . . . light the cabin and let him roast like pork. But he locked up his jaws and didn't say anything. A queer thing, Cameron. I was almost scared from just sittin' there and looking into the cold of his eyes. It almost made me think of hell, you know."

"And you went ahead," muttered Cameron.

"Wouldn't I have been a fool not to? I'd found the gold in the sacks. I needed that money, and needed it damn' bad. Old Peyton was too dead set against me marrying his girl unless I showed that I was able to take care of her. He said that he'd never put up the money for me to live easy. He's always seen through me a little. He's the only one of the Peyton family that has until you came along, damn you." There was no particular venom in this last speech. He shrugged his shoulders and went on: "Not that I give a damn about having Jacqueline wise to me. I never cared a rap about her. But I wanted her slice of the Peyton money when it came due. That old swine has a couple of millions. Know that?"

"I knew that he had money. Where did you kill the greaser?"

"You'd like to use that on me, wouldn't you? Why, it was a little side trip made down to Phoenix when I was a kid. If you live till tomorrow, you're welcome to use the news wherever you please."

Tierney laughed. He had a fine, mellow-sounding laughter, and the strength of it forced back his head.

"But damn the Peyton money," he went on. "I'll get along without it. I would have had to play a part with Jacqueline all my life, anyway, and I don't like to do that. Unless I decided to raise so much hell with her that the old man would buy me off with a good lump sum. I've never had to work my way, and I never will have to. Always too many suckers like you and Wayland. They dig out the coin, and the wise birds like me get it." He laughed again.

The brain of Cameron was spinning. "Tell me something, will you?" he asked.

"Sure. I'll tell you anything you want to know. It's the sort of pleasure that I've never had till now . . . talking what I please to a fellow who's going to be dead inside of a few minutes. It's like whispering secrets into a grave, kid." He began to laugh again, highly pleased by this thought.

"Well . . . tell me if you ever had a friend."

"Friends? I've had a dozen of 'em. Look at the two Peyton fellows. I've got the wool pulled over their eyes a yard deep. Sure I've had friends. I get a friend, use him, chuck him away. That's my idea. Now, let's talk business."

"What kind of business?"

"The way you're to die."

"There's the creek."

"You'd like that," agreed Tierney. "Sure you'd like it. But I want to have it longer and sweeter. Maybe you're not like Wayland. Maybe you'll pipe up some music for me, the same as the greaser did?"

"Maybe," said Cameron, through his teeth.

Tierney stood up and stretched. "Tell me something. D'you think you broke the skulls of both Harry and Joe?"

"No. They're only a little knocked out," answered Cameron.

"Too bad," murmured Tierney. "They're a pair of wooden dummies, and I'm tired of 'em. But what am I going to do about you, old son? I've got matches. How about lighting you up here and there and watching you roast? As long as you liked Wayland so much, you might as well go to hell the same way he went." He leaned over Cameron. "I think I'll have to take that pair of spurs, though," he decided. "Where'd you get golden spurs?"

"My friend gave them to me. Les Harmody."

"The hell he did. Why would Les be chucking away money on a 'breed like you?"

"He said it was to show that he thought I was as good as any white man."

"Did he? Well, you're not. Understand? When I've taken these spurs off, I'll show you what I think about you."

He leaned still farther. With an instinctive reaction, Cameron pulled his feet away, doubling his knees high.

"Good," said Tierney. "Going to be some struggling, eh? That's what I want. That's what I like. Put up a good fight, kid. I hate to hook a fish that won't do some wriggling. I'll have you screeching like the greaser on the barroom floor before I'm through with you."

He stepped forward to catch Cameron by one foot. His head was low. The target was not unattainable. And Cameron let drive with his heels at the head of Tierney—with the golden spurs of Les Harmody he struck out, making his supple body into a great snapping whiplash.

Tierney, seeing the shadow of the danger at the last instant, yelled out and tried to dodge. But the spurs tore across the flesh of his chin and the heels themselves thudded against the bone of his jaw. He fell on his face.

Cameron came to life, moving as a snake moves. He got the revolver from the holster at Tierney's side first. The big fellow already was beginning to move a little as Cameron held the weapon in both hands and with two bullets severed the wires that bound him at the knees and at the ankles.

It was a harder, an almost impossible, task to get a bullet through the wires that confined his two wrists. To manage that, he had to hold the Colt between his feet, pressing his wrists over the uptilted muzzle of the gun until one strand of the wire was against the muzzle of it. But he could not keep the flesh of the wrists from pressing over the muzzle together with the wires. He managed to get the middle finger of his left hand over the trigger of the gun, another extra pressure and the explosion followed. Hot irons seemed to tear the soft flesh inside his wrists—but his hands were free.

And there was Tierney on his feet at last, staggering a little, then snatching at a second gun as he realized what had happened. Cameron shot low, aiming between the hip and the knee, and saw the big fellow pitch to the side. He struck on both hands, the gun spinning to a distance. Then he reclined there as though he had been struck down by a spear and pinned to the ground.

"By God, it's not *possible*!" shouted Tierney. "Cameron, don't shoot . . . for God's sake, don't shoot."

Cameron went to the fallen gun and kicked it back to Tierney.

"I ought to cut you down and kill you the way you were going to murder me, Tierney," he said. "But I'm not going to do that. Wayland taught me a different way of living. There's the gun inside your reach. Grab it up. Fill your hand and take your chance."

"What chance? groaned Tierney. "I'm bleeding to death. Cameron, do something . . . help me. If you try to shoot it out now, I won't lift a hand. It'll be murder. It'll damn your soul to hell. For the sake of God, don't kill me."

"Look," said Cameron, "I'm sitting on the ground exactly like you now. I'm putting down the gun just the way yours is lying. Now fill your hand and fight . . . you yellow dog."

But Tierney, spilling suddenly forward along the ground, buried his face in his arms and began to groan for mercy.

Chapter Eight
White Man

That was why Cameron, his soul sick with disgust, brought Tierney into the town of Gallop with the feet of his prisoner tied under the belly of the horse. A crowd formed instantly. Men ran from the saloons, and some of these were sent off to rouse the doctor and prepare him for a trip.

Tierney, when he saw familiar faces, began to make a frantic appeal: "Bob . . . Sam . . . Bill . . . hey, Bill. Help me out of this. The damned 'breed shot me from behind. I'm bleeding to death. Bill, are you going to let me go like this?"

He held out his hands in appeal. Cameron rode beside him with no gun displayed. He made a picture that filled the eyes of men, however, and kept them at a distance. For blood had run and dried from a thousand scratches, and, naked as he was to the waist, he looked like a savage come back from war with a captive.

Harry Peyton and the gray-headed sheriff appeared at the same time, Harry shouting: "There he is, sheriff! There he is now. I'll help you get him."

Harry Peyton had a thick bandage around his head, but otherwise he appeared perfectly well. He was pulling out a gun as he ran. The sheriff stopped that.

"If there's any gun work wanted, I'll call for it," he said.

The crowd had become still thicker. Men held back from actually stopping the progress of Cameron, but they drew nearer and nearer.

"Are you the sheriff?" Cameron called out.

"I am," said the other, wading through the crowd.

"Then I'm turning Tierney over to you," said Cameron. "I'm charging him with the murder of Mark Wayland."

The sheriff came up, panting. Harry Peyton was at his shoulder, glowering, ready for battle. "You let me down, Harry, damn your heart," snarled Tierney.

"What's this charge of murder?" demanded the sheriff. "Are you wounded, Tierney? This looks like a damned black night's work for you, Cameron. Hold that horse. Harry, help me get Tierney off his horse. Cut that rope."

Now that the horses were stopped, the men pressed suddenly close from every side. There was a shout from the rear of the crowd: "Hang the damned 'breed! Lynch him!"

Cameron leaned from the saddle and gripped the shoulder of the sheriff. "Are you going to listen to me?" he demanded. And the green glare of his eyes struck a sudden awe through the man of the law.

"I'm listening to you," said the sheriff, scowling. "What's this talk about murder?"

"He killed Mark Wayland. He 'fessed it to me tonight."

"Confessed? What made him confess?"

"When he had me lying on the ground and tied with wire . . . the way he tied Wayland before he burned down the shack at the mine."

"What kind of a liar will you listen to, Sheriff?" demanded big Will Tierney. "He shot me from behind. . . ."

"Here's one proof," said Cameron, and he held out his wrists, with the blood still trickling from them, and the powder burns were horrible to see. The sheriff frowned and a curse of wonder escaped his lips.

"It's true," he said suddenly.

"You'll find the wound in his leg, whether he was shot from behind or not," said Cameron. "And if you want to know more than that, send down to Phoenix. They've wanted him for murder there for five years. They'll want him still."

He said it loudly, and the muttering of the crowd was blanketed in a sudden silence.

The sheriff said: "Look at me, Tierney. Is this true. Have you been a damn' wolf in sheepskin all this time?"

"Wait a minute!" yelled Tierney. "You wouldn't believe a 'breed against a white man's word, would you? You wouldn't . . . ?"

"Shut up," said the sheriff. "You're under arrest. Cameron, I can see that I've got to thank you for doing a job that I should have handled myself. Tierney, you look as guilty as hell, and hell is where you'll wind up, with a hangman's rope to start you on the way."

It may have been that the loss of blood and the successive shocks to his nerves had weakened Tierney, but, now, at the very moment when he should have rallied himself to make a last desperate appeal to the crowd that might have favored him, his nerve gave way. With one hand he gripped at his throat as though already he felt the rope about it, and slowly turning his head he stared at Cameron—a look that Cameron would never forget. Then they carried him toward the jail.

The sheriff lingered to say loudly: "The next man I hear calling Cameron a 'breed had better come and call me the same thing. There's no dirt on his skin that soap won't take off."

It was the same fellow who had yelled for a lynching who now started a new demonstration. Cameron marked him clearly. Perhaps, seeing how the wind was blowing from this unexpected quarter, the man wanted to bury his other remark under new fervor. But he it was who proposed cheers for Cameron, "who's all white," and the crowd, falling into the spirit of the thing, cheered itself hoarse and then trooped back into the saloons to start a celebration.

Cameron himself by that time was riding at the shoulder of the doctor, with Harry Peyton on the other side of him, and Joe Peyton in the rear. The brothers said nothing. They were not the kind to waste words, but neither, Cameron was sure, were they the sort to nourish grudges. And that was how they came back to the shack where big Les Harmody was lying.

When he heard them coming, Harmody shouted a question. Cameron's voice answered. And a cry of happiness broke from the throat of the wounded man.

There was not much need of talk. When Harry and Joe, who had started with Tierney, returned with Cameron and the doctor, it was a fairly clear proof that everything was altered in the affairs of Cameron. There was one anxious pause while the doctor made his examination of Harmody, then the medico looked up with a smile.

"Luck and an extra heavy set of ribs have saved you, Harmody," he said.

An involuntary gasp of relief broke from Cameron's lips, and, hearing that, Harmody held out a sudden great hand toward him.

"Old son," he said.

Cameron caught the hand and gripped it as hard as he could.

"The two of us, Les," he exclaimed.

"Fine," said Harmody. "But suppose we make it three?"

He looked across at the girl, and she, from her place beside the bed, forced her head up until she was looking with great eyes straight at Cameron. She began to smile in a way half fond and half foolish, and Cameron knew that he had reached the end of pain.

THE ONE-WAY TRAIL

The One-Way Trail

"The One-Way Trail" first appeared under the George Owen Baxter byline in Street & Smith's *Western Story Magazine* in the issue dated February 4, 1922. Even this early there are scenes and moments to be found in this short novel that clearly distinguish the kind of Western story written by Frederick Faust. There is action, motion, constant momentum, but the author's concern is not really focused on these but rather on what is most important and most intimate and most meaningful in our lives, what alone ultimately matters. Love, friendship, loyalty, courage are affirmed, yet beyond even these is the prospect of redemption. It comes about through human interaction in stories such as "The One-Way Trail" and the others collected here. They are not really plot-driven but depend on human character almost entirely for their motion and progression—the spiritual capacity for sublimity as well as despair, the potential for decency that exists in every human being, and the possibility even in the outcast, the criminal, the socially and politically disenfranchised to attain through one gratuitous act true nobility of soul.

Chapter One
Forced to Fight

The Shifter picked up a chair from the circle around the stove and, drawing it back a little so that no one could easily pass between him and the wall, he sat down to think. With The Shifter thinking was a process quite unusual. He ordinarily acted first and did his thinking afterward. Thinking was so strenuous a task that he needed utter repose of body while his mind struggled.

Not that The Shifter was stupid. Far from it. But he was only twenty-two years old and, though he had crammed enough action into that narrow span of life to furnish sufficient excitement to a dozen able-bodied men, he had never encountered a problem which could not be solved by the adroit use of his hundred and eighty-five pounds of mule-hard muscle. Or, if muscle alone could not gain the desired end, he possessed sundry accomplishments of wrist, finger, and eye which, in the parlance of the country, were termed collectively "gun sense." Consequently, it was not strange that The Shifter had not overstrained his mentality. But today it was different—very different.

He had come back to his home town of Logan expecting to be received with smiles and open arms as a hero. He had come back that morning after an absence of four years, during which he had not forgotten a single face or a single voice. But the applause which greeted him was so muted as to be almost non-existent. Old Curry, the town loafer, had greeted him to be sure with a broad grin and a request for a five-spot. But that was about the only smile he had encountered. A few minutes later the sheriff had come up to him—Sheriff Joe Brown who had taught him to ride in his childhood. He had been both curt and to the point.

"Now, look here, kid," he had said, "maybe you've come in all ready to light up and celebrate, but my job around these parts is to keep things quiet. You lay to that! And if they's any uncommon trouble starts, I ain't going to ask questions. I'll just start for you, Shifter, and start *pronto*."

With that, he had turned on his heel and strode off down the verandah. It was this that had made The Shifter go inside the hotel to find a chair and quiet so he could think. They were all against him. That was plain, and gradually he came to see why. They were afraid of him, afraid of The Shifter! He was like a stranger.

When they knew him as Harry French, before he went away, he had been as popular as any youth in the town. Now they seemed to think that he had changed his identity when he was given the nickname. They avoided his eye; they did not enter into conversation with him; and, when he entered a group, the group dissolved at once and reassembled in another place. He would not have been so surprised anywhere else, but here they ought to know him. They ought to understand that all the stories that floated through the mountains about him were not entirely true. He was a gunfighter only on occasion and by necessity, not by choice. Could not his own people see that at a glance?

He dropped his chin upon his hard, brown fist and pondered. His thoughts flickered out of the hotel lobby, stuffy from the heat of the stove and the closed doors and windows. They danced off to that day, four years before, when he had fought his first fight and won his nickname. It was in the mining town of Ferris to which Harry French had taken the optimism and the fine good humor of an eighteen-year-old youth.

There, on a pay night in the saloon, he had been involved without fault of his own in a sudden hurly-burly of fighting men. Somebody had chipped his ear with a bullet as he strove to get out of the sphere of danger. The moment Harry had felt the sting of the wound, he lost all desire to escape. He had turned back and rushed that crowd, weaving from side to side, smashing out with either hand, bowling over stalwart miners at every punch, until at length a panic took the crowd. They had bolted for the door. The town bully had remained, drawing his gun and Harry, avoiding the bullet with a side leap, had downed his man with a heavy slug in the thigh.

That was where he had earned the sobriquet of The Shifter because of the restless footwork with which he had gone through the mob. It was an instinct that made him do it. Ever after, when he entered a fight and rushed his man, he came swerving and dodging like a football player on an open field. The result of this swerving attack was that in all his fights he had never been touched with a bullet.

Others of those battles came back to his mind now. Certainly there were many of them—too many! His great consolation was that he had never picked trouble, never forced a combat. Trouble had simply hunted him down and forced itself upon him. And now they looked upon him, even these men of his home town, as little better than a legal murderer who picked fights and then used his uncanny ability to destroy his foes. That explained the cold glances he received. That explained why the little hush had fallen over the circle around the stove since he drew the chair back to the wall.

He raised his head. Every eye was fastened upon him, and instantly every glance turned in another direction. They did not wish to be found staring, for a gunfighter would pick a fight at the very slightest provocation. In fact, every one of those men, hardy fellows though they were, was sweating with anxiety as long as he was in their midst. What fools they were? Could they not see that his one consuming desire was to be friendly with them? Could they not see that he would pay for their esteem with combat?

Tears of vexation and self-pity rose to the eyes of The Shifter, and his scowl grew blacker as he studied the floor, looking down to hide that suspicious moisture. Footsteps entered, paused. The voices which had begun to murmur in conversation were solemnly hushed. The Shifter looked up to find a tall, raw-boned man staring at him with a face deathly pale. His hands were clenched to fists at his sides, and there was a set look of desperation about his face. The lips of the tall man worked a moment before sound came and, when he managed to speak, his voice trembled.

"You got my chair, French!"

Sudden understanding came to The Shifter. Here was Long Tom Cassidy, whom he had known like a brother four years before. Now Long Tom was ready to battle. The reason was perfectly clear. If an ordinary fellow had taken the chair, Tom would never have dreamed of raising an objection, for after all he had no power or right to reserve his seat when he left the room. It just happened that on this occasion, when he returned, he found every chair taken, and in his own recently abandoned place sat a killer of men. That was the reason he stood so straight and stiff. He felt that he would be shamed. He felt that he would be taking water if he allowed this terrible man to preëmpt his seat. Sooner than be shamed, Long Tom Cassidy was ready to die.

It came home to The Shifter of a sudden, and it made him sick at heart. What could he do? He would rather drive a bullet into his own flesh than shoot down Cassidy. But could he meekly rise from his rightful place and surrender it to another? Might that not be interpreted as disgraceful taking of water? Perhaps Cassidy had built up a reputation for skill with weapons in the past four years. Perhaps he might be capable of putting up a desperate battle, and the others would think that fear motivated The Shifter to make him move.

All these thoughts whirled in a blinding stream through the bewildered brain of The Shifter. He did not want to fight. His heart ached to go up and greet Tom with a hearty handshake, but he could not. Men would as soon shake hands with the devil. They sat about now staring with black brows from one to the other. Then, gradually, they began to shift their chairs out of the line between the two prospective combatants. Their sympathies plainly were all with Tom. At the least provocation they would join him against the gunfighter. The Shifter looked them over with the sad eye of despair and found not a single kindly response to his glance.

"You heard me talk?" Cassidy was saying, his voice gaining in strength and roughness.

"Tom," said The Shifter slowly, "don't be a fool. You ain't got this chair mortgaged, I guess?"

"Look here," cried Tom, "just save your words for them that'll stand 'em. I ain't your dog to be booted out of a chair and then jawed because I want it back!"

A spark of rage was fanned into a red gust of temper in The Shifter, a familiar red blur which had preceded all of his battles. But he controlled himself, leaning back in the chair and running the tip of his tongue over his white lips.

"Cassidy," he said, "you're hunting trouble. Cut it out. I'm not going to fight about a chair, even if you want to."

"Then," said Cassidy suddenly, "get out of it!"

The Shifter stared at the big man for a moment in silence, thinking harder than he had ever thought before. He decided to surrender. It was hard to do. It would bring doubt and some suspicion of cowardice upon him. But at least it would prove to the people of his own home town that he did not wish to force trouble on peaceful men. He leaned to rise.

What happened then was simply misapprehension and bad luck, though unquestionably the first movement of a man leaning to rise from a chair and the first movement of a man leaning to get at his gun are the same. At any rate Tom Cassidy, on edge with excitement, interpreted the movement in the second way and grabbed for his own gun.

That gesture The Shifter noted from the corner of his eye and saw that he would be forced to fight or die. His leap was of a tigerish speed. It carried him out of the chair and far to one side, where he landed with his gun in his hand. In the meantime the bullet from Cassidy's weapon had crashed through the back of the chair he had just left and dug through the wall behind. Long Tom whirled to fire again.

There was one alternative left to The Shifter and that was to run for the door. He would have done so had he not noted the effects of the first fire of Cassidy. The man was a little slow but terribly sure with his bullets. He would shoot The Shifter squarely through the middle of the back as his man went through the door. Flight would not do, then. Reluctantly, holding his fire to the last instant, The Shifter twitched up the muzzle of the gun which had been hanging idly at his side and fired.

Chapter Two
To Start Life Anew

In the pause that followed Long Tom Cassidy seemed like a very poor actor on the amateur stage. He did his gestures one by one with foolish awkwardness. The gun dropped from his hand and rattled on the floor. He gripped violently with both hands at his left thigh, and then he sank down on the opposite side.

The others had pressed back against the walls of the room with a shout. For an instant there was only the wail of the northern gale outside the hotel. Then the bystanders rushed in between and surrounded their fallen townsman. A quick examination of his wound showed that the bullet had passed through the flesh only, leaving bone and sinew untouched. He was carried from the room, groaning and cursing, just as the sheriff entered. As he had promised, he paused at the door only to jerk his hat lower over his eyes, then he went straight for The Shifter, a gun in either hand. As for The Shifter, he remained standing idly against the wall with the revolver hanging loosely from his finger tips.

"Stick up your hands, Shifter!" commanded the sheriff. "Stick 'em up!"

Only the muzzle of The Shifter's gun twitched up in return.

"I'll put 'em up when I get good and ready," he said slowly. "You, Brown, keep on the far side of the stove. Understand?"

"I'll make this the last fighting you do, bucko," growled the sheriff, but he remained on the far side of the stove.

The Shifter was white, as always, when he grew wildly

angry. "I used to think you were a man, Brown," he said. "But I see you ain't. They don't raise 'em that way around Logan. I come back here ready to act peaceable as a pet dog. First thing I know an idiot starts a fight about a chair. I leave it to the gents standing around here. Did I pick that fight?"

There was no answer.

"What?" shouted The Shifter. "D'you mean to say I started it?"

There was no answer.

"Wasn't I getting up out of the chair just they way he ordered me to do? Wasn't I taking water from him, when the hound pulled on me, and I had to jump to save my neck?"

But still from that circle of dour faces there was no response. The Shifter knew, at once, that he was beaten. He looked back at Joe Brown.

"Well, Sheriff," he said, "I see I get no backing. These blockheads can't see straight. If they do, they can't remember what they see. Point now is: what d'you mean to do?"

The doubt was all on the side of the sheriff. As for The Shifter, there was not a shadow of a doubt that he was enraged to the very verge of starting an attack. Many an old tale of his doings in battle floated back upon the memories of the others in the big room. If they wanted The Shifter, they could take him, but the price would be a terrible thing to pay. The sheriff ran his eyes around the circle and wondered. It might be that his reputation as a man-taker would be lost in this affair. But if the fight started, he himself would be the first target for that tall, gray-faced youth. It was a very convincing thought.

"I'll tell you what I'm going to do," said the sheriff, making his voice larger than his spirit. "I'm going to run you out of this town, Shifter. And I'm going to make it hot for you if you ever try to come back. If I had a shade more again' you, I'd lock you up now. But I figure Long Tom Cassidy made a fool play. Anyway, Shifter, out you go and on the run, too!"

The sheriff ran his eyes around the circle of listeners, and his heart warmed. There was an unmistakable air of relief on every face.

"I'll walk, Brown," answered The Shifter. "I was never built for running."

So saying, he deliberately shoved his revolver back into the holster, tilted his sombrero to a more rakish angle, settled his bandanna into a more flowing knot, and slowly sauntered across the floor with his pale-blue eyes wandering from side to side, daring them all, or anyone, to make the first move to detain him or to hurry him. But not a hand was lifted, not a voice was raised, until he reached the door and, with his back turned squarely toward them all, he opened it and stepped out into the staggering gale.

Then, inside the room, a loud buzz of comment rose. The younger men milled together, talking loudly of going after him and bringing him back, and they even went so far as to cast black looks of suspicion at reliable old Joe Brown. But the older men shook hands with the sheriff one by one.

"He didn't do enough for hanging," they assured Joe, "and it'd be a joke to put him behind the bars for anything else."

"He's sure gone bad," said the sheriff wisely, "and, if he shows himself around these parts again . . . well, I'll make things hum for that young man."

But The Shifter had not the slightest intention of ever showing himself within gunshot of Logan again. He was decidedly through. They, his own people, had denied him. They had refused to give him a chance or a hearing. They had set themselves shoulder to shoulder against him and, if he had not been hurt to the very heart, he could have laughed at their folly.

He went straight to the horse shed. A bony, Roman-nosed roan lifted an ugly head and glared at him above the side of the stall. The Shifter tossed a saddle over this unprepossessing beast and dug his knee into the ribs of the big horse as he tugged the cinches taut. Glorious—for that was the name of the homely brute, unless it were shortened to Glory—attempted to catch his master with a rear heel, tossed up with wonderful dexterity on the end of a long leg. Failing in this, he swung his head around but received an elbow in the nose as he attempted to sink his big teeth in the shoulder of the master. In another moment he was outside, bucking like a demon and running straight into the teeth of that terrific north gale.

Inside a quarter of a mile Glorious settled down to a long, easy canter, defying the force of the wind and even pricking his ears into it. In fact, Glorious was never so happy as when he was under way on a long journey and a hard one. His feud with his rider began with every saddling and ended with the first furlong or two of the gallop. For Glorious did not hate The Shifter in particular but mankind in general.

Out of a brief and terrible career as an outlaw in horse-breaking contests, he had passed into the capable hands of The Shifter, and he was gradually settling down. He had been long schooled to detest human beings, but the kindness of his owner was gradually neutralizing the acid in his disposition. The Shifter had found the long-legged brute invaluable. If there were savagery in the heart of Glorious, there was also uncanny wisdom in his brain. He could tell a rotten bridge by a glance and the first tentative tap on his forehoof. He knew by inborn instinct which stones on a mountainside would give sure purchase and which would roll at the first pressure. Mud or snow had no terrors for him. He could have kept his feet in a land-slide or have ambled easily on a trail well nigh too narrow for a man. Also, his fierceness was becoming very largely bluff. The Shifter had shrewdly guessed that in another six months, in spite of small eyes and Roman nose, Glorious would be as affectionate and trustworthy a mount as stepped through the mountains.

He drew the big horse down to a steady jog in anticipation of the long and hard trail that lay before them, for The Shifter intended to take the one-way trail across the Kendall Mountains to Vardon City. It was well-nigh a disused route. There were other trails across the mountains. The sole advantage of the one-way trail was that it was the shortest. Running down from the loftier peaks of the Vardon Mountains in the north, the Kendall River cut a narrow trench through the mountains of the same name, a gorge with sides as sheer as the walls of a room almost. Along one side of the gorge a difficult trail had been cut, dipping up and down, twisting in and out. In half a dozen places it was wide enough for passing, but mile after mile it stretched as a narrow little ledge where a man on foot was in danger and where a man on a horse continually risked his own neck and the life of his mount. In recognition of this fact there was an unwritten law that the trail should be used only by travelers from the south to the north to avoid any more head-on meetings such as had, in the early days, been the cause of more than one tragedy.

Ordinarily even The Shifter would not have thought of using this route, particularly now that the north wind was tearing through the gorge, ready to pry between the rider and the cliff wall beside him. But this was not an ordinary day for The Shifter. His mind was in a turmoil of rage, and he welcomed the prospective danger of the one-way trail as a relief. He only wanted to get out of his home town by the shortest and the most expeditious means, and consequently he directed the big, ugly head of Glorious toward the mouth of the gorge.

The wind was increasing steadily, stringing long, pale drifts of clouds across the sky, clouds in such rapid passage from the north that they flicked across the face of the sun in swift succession and dimmed it only momentarily, like a winking light. The Shifter bowed his head to the gathering force of the gale and rode on.

Behind him, about a mile away, came four horsemen, closely bunched and maintaining his own pace. When he halted, they halted likewise; when he cantered, they urged their horses into a gallop. It did not need much penetration to tell that these were townsmen come out to make sure that he was leaving that section of the country. The upper lip of The Shifter curled away from his teeth as he glanced back at them, and for a moment he felt one of those wild, hot impulses to turn his horse and charge back on them. But he restrained himself. No, his plan for life hereafter was to be free from violence. He would go into a section of the mountains where he had never been heard of, and there he would settle down and carve for himself the repute of an honest, patient, and law-abiding citizen. This idea was strong in his mind as he jogged up the last grade, turned about the shoulder of a mountain, and came suddenly upon the gorge of the Kendall River and the beginning of the one-way trail.

Chapter Three
A Stranger in a Hurry

It was unlike any other gorge he had ever seen. Though he remembered it well enough from the other days, it came upon him now like something seen for the first time. Other things had changed greatly in four years, but the one-way trail along the valley of the Kendall seemed more terrible than ever. The walls went upon either hand to the very summits of the range, as though the chain of the mountains had been stretched from each side until they snapped asunder along a smooth line of cleavage, or as though—to use an extremely old metaphor—a giant axe had cleft through a thousand feet of solid, virgin rock.

He looked down. The Kendall flowed through shadows, save where a shaft of sunlight was here and there reflected from the polished face of a cliff and brightened the water, and in those places he could make out the foam-white surface of that troubled water. When the shouting of the wind fell away from time to time, he heard the call of the Kendall go up the cliffs—wild voices snatched away a moment later in the renewed violence of the storm and blown to shreds. The trail was almost indistinguishable as it wound here and there, climbing with well-nigh imperceptible footings from one jutting crag to another. Sometimes it was merely a distant scratch along the blank walls of stone.

He looked back. The four watchers had bunched their horses closely together and were pointing after him apparently in great excitement. That decided The Shifter. He favored them with a deep-throated curse and then touched Glorious with the spurs. The big horse leaned far forward into the heart of the wind before he could take the first step, and then they jogged out onto the trail, with Glorious pressing close to the wall and snorting his fear of the dizzy fall on his right.

In half a mile he had lost his first terror and was giving himself to his work with consummate skill. The first sharp turn, following the winding of the valley, had proved nearly the death of both of them for, as they went about it, the storm smote them squarely from the inside, and Glorious tottered on the very edge of destruction. Only the quick action of the rider, as The Shifter flung himself violently to the left, gave Glorious a chance to regain his balance, and he found his footing once more. But that lesson did not need to be repeated. Thereafter he negotiated every turn of the trail like a seasoned diner-out approaching an unknown vintage. Glorious literally smelled his way to safety around every corner and then took the turn with his head lowered and his long, snaky neck stretched out. He made such a ridiculous appearance in the midst of this maneuver that Harry French several times burst into laughter. But Glorious merely shook his head and trudged on, regardless of the mockery.

As Madame du Deffand said, when she was told of the martyr who took ten steps after his head was struck off, it is the first step which is the hardest. Within ten minutes Glorious had negotiated all the variety of dangers which the one-way trail presented and had reduced his work to a perfect technique, the chief point being that at all times he kept his long body pressed closely to the wall even when the trail was comfortably broad.

Once his mount had gained this surety of going, The Shifter forgot to a great extent the dangers of the way. Even to the fierce pressure of the wind, now and again falling away and then striking at him with treacherous suddenness, the rider paid little attention. He almost lost himself in his thoughts. They ran, almost entirely, to the new life that would begin at the end of this trail. It was a melancholy series of reflections, taken all in all.

He felt that his past life was behind him, that twenty-two years had been wasted. When a boy reaches that age, he feels that a very great deal indeed has been passed. So The Shifter considered the future with a gloomy sobriety of mind. Out of his past every remembered face was a dead thing, every remembered voice was a ghost.

The Shifter was brought out of these dreary reflections, these grave plans for the future, by a sharp prick of reality. He turned a corner of the trail with his head bowed into the teeth of the wind, and he did not raise it again until he was astonished by the stopping of Glorious. Then he looked up and found facing him a youthful rider on a big, brown horse. And the trail was not three feet wide!

Even two men, in passing, would have leaned in against the wall, so dizzy was that fall which must be avoided. It was impossible for even the most adroit and cat-footed mustang to turn in this space. For horses as large as Glorious and the brown, it was absurd to attempt such a maneuver. Neither could they back the horses to a possible turning place, for behind each was the bend which had just been rounded. If the horses could barely make way around those turns going ahead, it would be an insured fall if they were forced against instinct to back up around them. Besides, it might be a mile in either direction before a more advantageous position were reached.

Both The Shifter and the other sat their horses in silence, drinking in the full extent of the catastrophe, while the animals swayed a little from side to side under the outrageous cuffing of that north wind. The Shifter adjusted himself in the saddle, so that that cunning right hand of his would be perilously near the holster and ready for use, while he studied the stranger. The man was apparently between twenty-five and thirty, perhaps even more. He was well built, rather stocky and broad shouldered, compared to the athletic ranginess of The Shifter, but brown with outdoor life and sufficiently deep of chest to promise unusual power in a hand-to-hand effort.

The head, however, was not so formidable as the body. It was distinctly small, and the face was small likewise, with handsome features extremely regular in cut and oddly contrasted with the aquiline cast of The Shifter. The eyes, too, were set closely together, and in their restless quality they suggested a certain unhealthy cunning that troubled The Shifter.

Yet, whatever the physical possibilities of the stranger, he was now in a blue funk. Never had The Shifter seen a man so obviously in the grip of the frozen hand of terror. He sat in his saddle with mouth agape, staring, his face bloodless. When he attempted to speak, Harry French made out only a meaningless gibberish.

For one thing, it plainly declared to The Shifter that he was the master of the situation. This trembler would make no stern opposition to his will and his ways. But also it was a thing so disgusting to watch that The Shifter blinked and looked away. He was embarrassed also. Some hard-faced, formidable man would have been preferred to this coward, for then they could have fought it out. The better man would have gone on.

"Well," asked The Shifter, "what d'you make out of this business? What'll we do?"

"What do I make out of it?" the other shrilly called back, his face reddening with anger as suddenly as he had grown pale. "What I want to know is what you mean by riding up this trail in the face of a wind like this? Are you crazy?"

The Shifter paused a moment before he answered. He had been vowing, in his inward thoughts of the moment before, that hereafter he would take plenty of time before he spoke or acted. Now he began to act accordingly.

"Seems to me," he said mildly, when he had regained mastery of that treacherous temper of his, "that I'm the one that has the right to ask questions. This here is a one-way trail, I guess. I'm riding it the right way, and you're riding it the wrong way. Got anything to say to that?"

The other hesitated. Then he answered authoritatively: "Plenty to say. I'm in a hurry. I got to get to the end of the gorge. That's why I'm riding this way."

"Same way with me," said The Shifter, his anger steadily rising in spite of himself. "I'm riding this trail because I'm in a hurry."

"In a hurry!" cried the other, and his face swelled with red passion. "In a hurry . . . so you buck into a wind like this! Why, it was all me and my hoss could do to keep to the trail with the wind behind us. In a hurry!"

He regarded The Shifter with a fierce contempt, and the younger man closed his eyes for an instant and commended his heart of hearts to patience. In his entire life he had never met with a man who so keenly aroused his hatred.

"Look here," he said coldly, "they's one thing plain. These two hosses can't get by each other. I'm not saying who's to blame for it. But I'll give you a fair break. One hoss has to die and drop down into the Kendall River. No other way out. The other hoss goes on through, and the gent that loses has to finish his trip on foot. We'll throw a coin, partner, to see who loses and who keeps his hoss."

So saying, he drew forth a broad, half-dollar piece and juggled it in his hand. But his heart was by no means as light as his manner. There was not a sinew in the big, ugly, powerful body of Glorious that The Shifter did not love. Only there was nothing else to be done.

"Throw a coin to see which hoss dies?" The stranger sneered as he spoke. "Say, friend, d'you think I'd risk a hoss like The General, here, against a skinny old ramshackle like your roan?"

"You've said a tolerable pile," said The Shifter through his teeth. "And you've said a pile too much. If you got talking to do, try out your tongue on something beside my hoss."

The other changed his manner at once. "In a way," he said with a lofty condescension, "I'm in the wrong, and I've

175

brought this mess about. Well, I'll pay you the price of your hoss. I'll pay you a good price, too."

The Shifter smiled. "D'you think a hoss means just so much money to me?" he asked. "Why, stranger, a hoss is a life, just the way you and me are lives. You can't buy a hoss. You may pay somebody a price, but you ain't paying the price to the hoss. A pile of gents sit the saddles on hosses that they don't own a hair of, because they ain't never taught the hoss to love 'em."

"Bah!" snorted the other. "You talk plumb ridiculous. This is my hoss, got my brand on him, bought with my money. He's just hossflesh. To be used, like soap or oil or coal."

"All right," said The Shifter, breathing hard, "maybe that's all he is to you. I'm sorry."

"For what?"

"For the hoss."

"What d'you mean?" exploded the stranger, pushing his brown horse closer to The Shifter.

But he got no farther in his tirade. The Shifter suddenly swung forward in his saddle, clinging with trembling knees to the sides of Glorious, and his face was gray and drawn. Save for his eyes, he seemed to be in a panic, but the eyes bore an ample assurance that he was in a red fury. The stranger shrank, and his own eyes grew dim and wide.

"Now talk business," said The Shifter. "Shall I throw the coin?"

"All right . . . all right, if it's got to be that way. But lemme get close enough to see the coin fall."

So saying, he pressed nearer, until the head of the brown was near that of Glorious, and on the inside. What was about to come The Shifter had no means of guessing save that, as he took the half dollar on top of his thumb, preparatory to snapping it into the air, he saw that the hand of the stranger on the bridle rein was trembling and gripped hard.

He snapped the coin high, raised his head to watch its twinkling rise and, just when it hovered brightly at the height, the brown horse was driven at him by a yell of the stranger. He was perfectly helpless. With head thrown up, urged on by the driving of the spurs in his tender flanks, the brown came in with maddened eyes, driving between Glorious and the cliff.

Chapter Four
Charged with Capital Crime

There was no time to whip out a gun and shoot, no time to fling himself from the saddle, no time even to throw his weight in toward the cliff to steady Glorious, for the rush of the brown forced the roan straight up and back, rearing and toppling on his hind legs, while the voice of the other rider, yelling with savage satisfaction, urged the brown on. The Shifter looked down. Far below him, with nothing between, rushed the Kendall. The upward and backward lurch of the roan was driving him swiftly to the toppling point. Already, he was clinging fiercely with his knees to keep from pitching headlong out of the saddle.

He saw, to the side and before him, the convulsed face of the stranger as he pressed the brown in and, with his quirt, showered stinging blows over the head of the roan. Glorious, with a squeal of rage and fear and pain, rocked and balanced erect as a bear on his hind legs. The one great forehoof went up, flashed down. Again and again and again! He was fighting as wild stallions fight, not submitting tamely to destruction. To escape that crushing, slashing shower of blows, the brown horse in turn reared, a maneuver which brought a yell of terror from the stranger. The Shifter, at the same instant, flattened himself along the neck of Glorious and gave weight to the rush as the roan drove forward on all four legs and now charged like a fighting dog at the throat of the brown.

Higher the brown reared, to strike with battering forehoofs even as Glorious had done, but Glorious drove in like a savage terrier, and now the weight of his shoulder ground in between the brown and the cliff. There was a shriek from the stranger as the brown reeled back. The Shifter, realizing that their rôles had been changed, struggled furiously at the reins to draw Glorious back, but it was like tugging at a stone wall. Higher went the brown, staggered, and, with a terribly human scream of fear, pitched sidewise into the abyss. The Shifter caught a glimpse of a face hideous with terror, the lips writhed back over a shriek which did not come. Then he swayed far out in the saddle, reached with both hands, and with the right he caught the falling man by the shoulder.

The whole length of that arm was whipped through his grip, the sleeve being torn away like cobweb under the terrific force of his hand. But the strain checked, in a measure, the impetus of the fall and, as his right hand caught a firm hold on the wrist, The Shifter flashed his left across and secured a hold lower down. The whole weight of the falling man came with a single jerk—for all of this, of course, happened inside a tenth part of a second—upon the strained shoulders of The Shifter. Glorious, swung over by the sudden side strain against which he could not brace himself, toppled on the very verge of the cliff. Snorting with fear, he fought to regain his balance and, looking down, The Shifter found himself suspended for the second time over the gulf of the cañon. He might throw away his life and the life of his horse for the sake of a man who, he knew, was a treacherous cur. But the sight of that fear-frozen face hanging there a double-arm's length away made him retain his hold. Never had he passed through such a moment. The opening of his hand would save himself and send another human being to death.

Then Glorious, struggling hard, caught his balance again and swayed toward the face of the cliff. In a moment the crisis was over, and the stranger lay senseless on the floor of the trail beside the roan. The Shifter himself was trembling like an invalid newly risen from bed when he climbed slowly out of the saddle and kneeled above the rescued stranger. One pressure of his hand assured him that the fellow lived, though the heart beat faintly and the lungs merely stirred. The Shifter rose, climbed into the saddle again, and pressed slowly on down the trail, speaking in a shaken and changed voice to Glorious. He could not force himself to stay until the stranger returned to his senses. He could not stay to hear thanks from the lips of this detestable coward.

After that the trail seemed as broad and as safe as a high road. What matter if the wind were increasing? What matter if the evening were coming on? What matter even if the rain began to whip out of the sky and rattle against the slicker which he put on? All of this was nothing. If Glorious slipped on a wet stone in the dimness and reeled on the verge of the precipice, it was almost a thing to be laughed at, for The Shifter and his horse had seen the very face of death that day on the trail, and now nothing mattered.

It took more than two hours to do the remaining six miles of the trail, with all of its ins and outs and ups and downs and hardly a place where they could do better than walk. The rain was coming down in streams of stinging force through the dull twilight when The Shifter rode into the muddy streets of Vardon City and heard the downpour drumming heavily on the roofs on either side, while the light from the windows was split into yellow sprays in passing through the torrent of rain. It seemed to The Shifter a harborage and a refuge of perfect peace after the terrors of the one-way trail. He secured a room at the hotel without difficulty and went up to it at once to lie down to rest—to rest and to think for, oddly enough, his first step into a life of kindliness had almost brought him to his death.

He lay on the bed with his eyes closed wearily, and through his mind passed the picture of what the other Harry French would be doing at this moment, the other Harry French who had existed that very morning. He would be down in the lobby of that old building holding the center of the stage with his stories, with his laughter, with his mockeries. He would be beating down the glances of quieter men with his own defiant

180

and bold eyes. After all, was it not better to live like that, to be feared and respected and followed and admired even by those who dared not imitate him? Was it not better than to lie here in the darkness brooding over what the future might hold for him?

He rose drowsily to answer a soft tap at the door. He swung it wide. There in the hallway stood a middle-aged man in an immensely wide-brimmed sombrero and, behind him, solidly packed, were half a dozen more. Every eye was focused on the face of The Shifter with an intensity with which he was bitterly familiar. The leader planted his riding boot inside the door so that it could not be closed. His right hand rested prominently on the butt of his revolver.

"You're Harry French?"

"Who are you to ask?"

"I got a right to ask questions, son. I'm the sheriff, John Clark."

The thoughts of The Shifter danced away into the obscurity of strange reflections. Since his resolution to lead a peaceable life he had been forced into a brawl by a man he tried to avoid, had been driven from his own home town, had been nearly murdered on a mountain trail, and now a sheriff with a formidable posse was invading his hotel room to ask him questions.

Sheriff Clark who, of course, could not follow the trend of these thoughts was astonished to see The Shifter burst suddenly into ringing laughter. Then the latter drew back politely.

"Come in, gents, and make yourselves to home. Sorry I ain't got anything to offer you to drink. But I ain't a drinking man, and I hate moonshine, anyways."

"Gunfighters and card sharps mostly do," said the sheriff. With this insult on his lips, he kicked the door still wider and strode into the room with his men packed behind him.

As for The Shifter, he saw that a side leap would take him to his gun and belt where they lay on the bed, and then it would be a comparatively simple matter—for him—to jump through the window onto the roof of the shed beneath and so down to the ground and only a few steps from the horses. From the entrance speech of the sheriff he gathered that the visit foreboded him no good. Or were they simply about to invite him to leave the town and ride on?

The sheriff was walking slowly around the room. He reached the gun belt and picked it up.

"I'll keep this a while," he said and drew the gun from the holster.

That is, he made the beginning of a movement to take the weapon, but the gesture was never completed. The toe of The Shifter's boot at that instant connected with the sheriff's wrist, drew a curse of pain and surprise from that worthy, knocked the gun spinning into the air and, when it descended, it fell into the agile hand of The Shifter.

He stood with his back to the wall, with a semicircle of armed men before him, every man ready to shoot. Again The Shifter could have laughed, if it had not been for the fierce and rebellious pain in his heart. For the second time on the first day of his good resolutions he found the protectors of social quiet arrayed *en masse* against him with their guns in their hands.

The sheriff was nursing his injured wrist with his other hand, still cursing, but he showed no fear, it must be admitted in his favor, and barked forth a steady series of orders to his men. "Watch that window, Bud and Joe. It opens out over the roof of the shed. Block the door, Charlie. And just light that lamp, will you, Pete? We need more light than what we get out of the hall. There's plenty of time to get his gun."

"Sure," said The Shifter coolly. "A sheriff can have my gun any time for the asking but not for the taking."

"Why, you fool," retorted the sheriff, while the flame welled up in the chimney of the lamp as Pete lighted it, "d'you know you've resisted arrest?"

"You lie," said The Shifter almost wearily. "Nobody's told me I'm under arrest. You started to grab my gun, and I kicked it out of your hand. I'd do it again. Keep off there, you with the red hair! You can go as far as the law allows you but, if you take a step farther, I'll singe your whiskers for you!''

This last was addressed to a big man who started to edge in along the wall. His progress was instantly arrested.

''You see?'' said the sheriff. ''I told you what he was! All right, Shifter. I'll tell you now that you're under arrest.''

''That's easy to say,'' answered The Shifter calmly. ''But what's the charge? You can't railroad me, partner.''

''The charge is murder on the one-way trail,'' said the sheriff, his voice suddenly trembling with emotion. ''Murder of my son, Jack Clark!''

Chapter Five
In the Vardon City Jail

The pale-blue eyes of The Shifter narrowed as he stared at the sheriff, but there was no similarity between that brown, hard-featured countenance and the face of the man he had drawn back from the peril of falling into the chasm of the Kendall River.

"Murder?" repeated The Shifter calmly. "Murder of a gent on a brown horse . . . big-shouldered fellow with a sort of smallish head and a . . . a foolish face?"

The sheriff clamped his teeth together. "You hear him, boys?" he said to the others. "He's identified Jack! I've found 'em cold-blooded and steady as iron before but never as bad as this."

There was a murmur of assent from the others.

"He's not dead," said The Shifter. "He's out on the one-way trail."

The sheriff shook his head. "You save that talk for the judge. Meantime, will you give up your gat peaceable?"

"Partner," said The Shifter as calmly as ever, "I never play a game that's sure to be a loser. Here it is."

He handed over the weapon. There was a general sigh of relief from the others.

"Hold out your hands," commanded the sheriff and then, over The Shifter's readily proffered wrists, he snapped the handcuffs.

"What you say'll be remembered for the jury and the judge," he said, "but if you want to talk, go ahead. We'll all listen . . . and we'll all remember."

"D'you think," said The Shifter, "that I'd've let you get me so dead easy if I was afraid my yarn wouldn't hold? I'll tell you the straight of it. I was coming north along the trail and at about the middle of it, while I was bucking a hard wind, I come on a gent riding the wrong way. There wasn't no chance to pass, and there wasn't no way of getting to a turning place except by backing one of the hosses about a mile. You know that couldn't be done on the one-way trail with the wind blowing the way it was today. They was only one way out and that was to kill one of the hosses and let it fall over the cliff. By rights, him traveling the wrong way, his hoss had ought to've been killed. But I offered to toss a coin for it and, while I was throwing the coin, this yaller-hearted skunk that you say is your boy rode his hoss at me and tried to knock me over the cliff, and he damned near done it. But old Glorious up and beat him off with his forehoofs and then jumped for the throat of the brown hoss like a fighting dog. I tried to pull him in, but it wouldn't work. He had the bit. And he jammed the brown hoss right off the trail. They fell together, your son and the hoss. . . ."

There was a deep groan from the sheriff.

"But I grabbed him as he was falling," went on The Shifter hastily, "and I pulled him back onto the trail. He fainted plumb away from the scare. I made out that his heart was still beating, and then I rode on down the trail. And that, gents, is the straight of the story, I swear it! Either he's in Logan by this time, or else he's still on the trail."

There was something so convincing about the manner in which this story was told, incredible though some of the mentioned incidents were, that the men of the posse looked from one to the other after the fashion of men whose conviction has been shaken and who are willing to hear more reason. But the sheriff, though his eye had brightened, shook his head.

"We'll give you the chance, son," he told The Shifter. "We'll send a man to ride the trail, and we'll wire down to Logan to see if Jack has come in yet. But the fact is that Jack has had plenty of time to of got to Logan long before this. Soon as I had word that the fool boy had took the one-way trail in the wrong direction, I wired on ahead to Logan and asked if anybody had entered the trail from that end. I got back word right off that you were just starting up that way. Well, Shifter, next we heard was that Jack's brown hoss had come rolling and tumbling down the Kendall, all smashed to pieces. But no Jack had come through. Then we see you big as life riding out of the one-way trail. And you didn't have no story to tell till just now. Why didn't you talk out as soon as you come in? Wasn't it worth talking about?"

The Shifter shrugged his shoulders. "Go ride the trail," he said calmly. "You'll find him. You can leave me in the lock-up till he's located. I guess that's square all around?"

Everyone had to agree that it was. They took Harry French—still following him in a compact body as though even his manacled hands were to be feared—downstairs to the street and up the street through the crashing rain to the edge of the village. Here they turned to the left and approached, down a graveled road winding among trees, a house larger than any other which The Shifter had seen in Vardon City. But when he came close under it, he suddenly remembered many things out of his boyhood and particularly this building, so large that it could be seen from the head of the Kendall Gorge, big among the little shacks of the town.

It turned out to be the home of the Clarks which also served as the town jail. The stout cellar wall offered a greater security than any other building in the town and saved the village the expense of a public structure. To the sheriff himself it was a double advantage, for on the one hand he received a generous fee for lodging the guests of the county and, on the other, the fact that he owned the jail was a sort of automatic assurance that he would be reëlected to the office of sheriff so long as he cared for the position.

Through a hall of mid-Victorian magnificence The Shifter was conducted to a door which opened on a flight of dark, damp stairs, and down this he was brought to the jail proper. A fencing of steel bars had been constructed like a great netting throughout the cellar and was divided and subdivided into a dozen cells, though more than half of that number had never been occupied at one time. At the present moment there was not a single tenant on any of the little cots. The Shifter was assigned to the central cell which had the advantage of offering him no concealment from spying eyes. Moreover, in case he attempted to break out, he would have two barriers of steel bars to cut through instead of one. All of these facts the sheriff pointed out to his companions who wandered about here and there admiring the interior of the jail with a sort of proprietary pride.

"There ain't any town of our size in the mountains that can show a better jail or a safer jail," they declared more than once, and the sheriff smiled with becoming modesty as he unlocked the door and ushered The Shifter into his place of confinement. One of them came back to The Shifter when the party was about to leave and, leaning against the bars, he nodded wisely to the prisoner from whose hands the manacles had, of course, been removed.

"We know you, French," he said. "We remember you from the days before you got to be known as The Shifter. Maybe you've turned out bad . . . as bad as we've heard. And maybe you ain't so bad, after all. But you can lay to it that you'll get a square deal in Vardon City. Here's wishing you good luck."

The Shifter shook hands heartily through the bars.

"I'll tell you what," he said, "Vardon City ain't through with me. I'm about to settle down, partner, and I've made up my mind that I'll settle down right here. If you folks don't like me to start with, I'll make you like me before I'm through."

The other grinned. Then he whispered shyly: "Don't let the sheriff get you worried so you try to bust out. He's just nacheral gloomy. You see?"

With this word to the wise and a broad wink, the good-natured fellow left The Shifter to his thoughts and retired to retreat with the rest of the party. Alone with the cellar dimly illumined by the light from a single lantern which swung from a rafter in a corner, The Shifter immediately set about examining his surroundings. He had entered the jail in perfect confidence but, when he heard the steel-barred door slam behind him and heard the heavy lock click, his heart had leaped into his throat, as it does when one jumps into cold water. He was trapped, and no matter how harmless his actions had been, the fact that he was helpless was in itself alarming. The size of the lock on the door made him yearn for a key to open it, in spite of his good intentions to let the law take its own course in its own way.

In the meantime his cautious explorations revealed several things of interest: that the bars which surrounded him were new and unrusted, that they were thick and set close together and resisted his grasp and strong pull, as though each were a wall. Above and on every side he was hemmed in by a resistless opposition. He lifted with ease one of the broad, thin boards which formed the flooring of the cell and found what he had dreaded to find—that the network of steel bars ran under the boards. Truly, he was securely held, and the thought sent a numb thrill of uneasiness into his brain.

Suppose something happened to Jack Clark on the one-way trail? Suppose, in the downpour of rain, his foot had slipped on a wet rock, or in the dimness of twilight he had fallen and . . . ? But here The Shifter's brain refused to work any further with the grim possibility. Upon the known safety of Jack Clark depended his own life. So much was clear.

He had lain down and composed himself for sleep when this possibility entered his mind and brought him bolt upright on his cot. As he sat there with his head in his hands, he was suddenly startled by a feeling that someone was nearby, watching. He looked up with a jerk and found that the sheriff had stolen into the cellar, his footfalls covered by the noise of the storm which still yelled and drummed outside the house. He stood in uncanny silence, his face pressed close to the bars, his eyes on fire with savage hatred. The Shifter, cold with dread, straightened slowly to his feet.

"Well?" he asked, so dry of throat that he could hardly speak.

"We've wired to Logan again," said the sheriff. "Jack ain't there."

"He's on the trail, then," said The Shifter, gripping his hands and steeling himself to fight away the convulsive shudders which were spreading over him.

"We've rode the trail. We've had 'em ride all the way up from Logan. Jack ain't on the trail."

"Then where is he?"

"Down in the Kendall River where you throwed him when you killed him!"

"Sheriff . . . !"

"I'll see you swing for it," said the sheriff slowly. "Aye, I'll see you swing for it. You've sent him to his death. You've sent me to mine. And I'll see that you go down with us. Sleep on that!"

He turned and stalked from the room with a long, slow stride but with his shoulders sagging, as though all in a moment an irresistible load of years had been poured upon him.

Chapter Six
A Decision Is Reversed

The stairs from the cellar to the first floor creaked one by one, one by one, under the step of the sheriff. Between every sound his mind rushed through years of life, years of planning and of hope which had been blasted this night by The Shifter. He had built his own future on the future of his son; with his son gone, his own hopes of success were withered at the root. Not that the heart of the grim man was tender for his offspring. He knew the boy for what he was—a coward, a knave by instinct, and something of a fool. But, nevertheless, he had planned to wrest success and wealth from the world through the use of this wretched tool, and he had been on the verge of victory when the tool was torn from his hands. That was why his eyes were fiery when he leaned at the bars of The Shifter's cell and looked at him.

It was an unsavory story, that tale of his life's plans. Ten years before, rich William Chalmers had died and left his daughter and sole heir in the keeping of John Clark as guardian. The fortune which went with her had been tied up in bonds—all but a small sum for her living expenses—and the very interest upon them could not be touched until Alison Chalmers reached her eighteenth birthday. The sheriff had taken the custody of the child with the best of intentions and in all good faith. The gradual wreckage of one business scheme after another did not alter him. Another man would have seen a chance of escape in the fortune which the girl held as her own, but the sheriff was not of that kind of stuff. He had no idea of using the fortune of the girl with or without her will.

True, he did conceive the idea of marrying Alison to his son, but he conceived it without malice aforethought. It is true too that, even as he planned the thing, he knew that his son was really unworthy of the girl, but in Alison he also saw the salvation of Jack Clark. Other fathers had made the same mistake before him.

Although at times he might shrewdly have guessed that his son was a coward and a knave, as a rule he closed his eyes to the truth and strove to make himself think that Jack only needed the passage of time to make him into a real man. He could not be wrong. The boy's mother had been a gentle wife whom the sheriff still loved and looked back on with a deep devotion. The sheriff had never been accused of cowardice or of the instincts of a bully.

More than once the very flesh of John Clark had crawled when he heard or saw evidence of the mean spirit of his boy, but always he shook his head and returned to reasoning and self-delusion to cover up the fact. It was sad, and it was shameful, but, after all, it was natural. He could not despise his own son. Jack must be a good man—in the making. The sheriff would do what he could. When he was done, he depended upon the girl to come to his aid and finish the job.

There was one great, almost insuperable obstacle. Alison hated Jack. More than once this fact had made the sheriff draw back from his plans and shake his head. He wanted the girl to be happy. He wanted to secure her future just as much as her own father could have wished it, but what he could not eventually see was that happiness could never be based upon bed rock if she were to be married to his son. Middle-aged people have a strong predisposition toward believing that the ideas of the young are changeable. Time will tell the tale is too often their creed. And that was the creed to which the sheriff held. Time would change Jack, and time would also change the girl. He himself would oversee the marriage and make sure that

Jack treated Alison well. Under his oversight he did not see how matters could go wrong.

He forgot his own youth. He forgot a young man's opinion of marriage. Love was something which he left out of his estimate in the full assurance that habit could take its place. The bitter truth is that men who have loved their wives are too apt to think that a man *must* love a good woman and that a woman can grow accustomed to any man.

All of these things John Clark had pondered upon many, many times. He was struggling honestly to do the right thing throughout. That struggle occupied a great many of his waking hours. There was only one point in his conduct in which he was dubious. That point was whether or not it was right to hold Alison back from communion with other boys and girls of her age. On this subject he debated with himself long and earnestly. His conclusion was wrong, but it was a conclusion honestly reached and honestly maintained. Many and many a time he had said to himself it was fitting that Alison have the right to her own society among the young people of Vardon City, and he knew that she would quickly become popular among them. But he knew also that, pretty as she was, she would be very apt to be impressed with one of the youngsters of the town. This must not be. It was cruel to keep her at home, but by keeping her at home he swore to himself that he was reserving her for an assured happiness when she should marry Jack and when she should achieve the position of head of a happy household under his own supervision.

No doubt this was blind argument. No doubt it was folly. But the sheriff was honest in his conclusions. The result was that he kept her at home, saddling her with household duties above her years. He knew it was painful to her. But he promised himself that in the future she would be amply rewarded for the pain which she now underwent. After the marriage—why, her life would start anew. In the meantime he kept her closely at home. After the days in the public school were finished—and he was glad when they were ended—the sheriff saw to it that she left the house very seldom. He discouraged all intimacy between her and the young men of Vardon City. If he needed an excuse, he found it readily.

"She's not very well," he used to say to people. "You see how pale she is."

All the time he knew that the pallor, the silence, the downward-cast eyes, were the result of his own regime which he imposed upon her. The full realization of this struck him when he stepped through the door to the hallway. There was Alison carrying a lamp in one hand and a tray of food in the other for the prisoner. He had not heard her coming. It was characteristic of her, this softness of foot. She stole through the house like a phantom, never lifting her eyes even when she was spoken to, even when she answered.

Bitterly the sheriff realized that this was his work. He saw her now for the first time as he stared at her in the dim hallway. How pretty, indeed! There was a woman who would make some man happy. Possibilities of warmth of soul and of manner were in her. Almost against his will he had checked and changed those impulses. He should have given her freely to the companionship of those of her own age. He had not done so, and for that reason he felt that he had done a hard and cursed thing. Well, now had come the time when he would make amends, most generous amends.

He loved the girl. Many a time he had had to pretend a harshness with her in order to give instructions that kept her at home at her drudgery. But all of those instructions had been for the sake of Jack and, now that Jack was gone, all was changed. Jack was gone, and there remained only one cause for his living. That was to make life happy for the daughter of his old friend. In his sad heart he felt a store of inexhaustible tenderness. How astonished she would be when he began to draw upon that store and pour it forth upon her.

Curiously, sadly, he gazed upon her. She was like a new creature, considered in this different perspective. Yet, he was bothered by those downward eyes. She did not lift them when she saw him but came to a patient halt in enduring silence. Sight of that pale face with the purple-shadowed eyes fell like a whip on the soul of the sheriff. It was his work, and how completely it was his work, only he could tell. But he would make amends, now that Jack was dead and his hopes undone. He would make amends in some way. With that good thought a chain was burst somewhere in his heart. Tears rushed to his dry eyes, tears which the loss of Jack had not brought.

"Alie, dear . . . ," he began.

Her eyes rose. She cast on him a glance of utter astonishment, utter fear, and shrank a little to one side as though to give him more room for passing her. She was used to curt commands, and this caress in his voice startled her. The sheriff turned and stumbled blindly down the passage. He heard the cellar door close behind her as he reached the stairs.

Now he needed quiet to think matters over and rearrange the scattered remnants of his hopes. So he trudged up the stairs to the second story to seek his little private office. He lighted a match as he entered, fumbled until the lamp jingled under his hand, and then lighted it. As he replaced the chimney, his left hand froze about the glass, for he was acutely conscious of another presence in the room. Then he whirled with his hand on his gun and looked straight into the grinning face of his son.

So completely had he made up his mind that the boy was dead that now he blinked in a ghostly fear. Then he straightened, caught Jack by the shoulders, and shoved him with a low cry of rejoicing against the wall.

"Hey!" cried Jack, writhing in that iron grip. "Let go, will you? Let go. I ain't made of leather. What's all the fuss about?"

The sheriff stepped back, still choking with relief and happiness. "We gave you up. What happened, Jack? How come you to get out of the trail? Did you fly? We got a gent down in the cells that I was getting ready to have hung . . . and here you pop up with a dry skin.'' He laughed, his voice trembling with pleasure.

''A gent on a roan hoss?'' asked the son.

''That's the one.''

''I wish you'd hang him, anyway,'' Jack went on surlily. ''He was the cause of killing the brown, and he near killed me, too. Tried to ride between me and the wall. He done it, too, and pushed the brown over the cliff. I jumped just in time, but I hit my head against the rock. When I come to, he was gone, and it was getting dark. So I turned and got back here without nobody seeing me. But . . . you don't have to turn that skunk loose, do you?''

The sheriff nodded. ''No matter what happened, it was your fault. You had no call to ride the one-way trail south.''

''Who'd've thought they was such a fool in the world as to ride that trail north ag'in' such a wind? Anyway, I was in a hurry.''

The sheriff sat down, mopping his forehead clear of perspiration, though the room was cold. He said weakly: ''It seems all like the insides of a dream. I'm just waiting to wake up. But what made you in such a hurry?''

The eyes of Jack glanced, ferret-like, from side to side. ''I told you I had to have that three hundred,'' he said sullenly. ''I did have to have it. It was a matter of life and death!''

''Three hundred!'' cried the father angrily. ''Where'm I to get three hundred every time you turn around. You spend more'n I do the way it is. What made it a matter of life and death? Whose life and death?''

''Mine!''

The father stared. ''Yours? What you been up to? What you been doing, Jack? I know you've played the skunk more'n once, but I never knew you had the nerve to do something that needed killing to pay you back.''

Under the stream of sarcastic abuse, the lip of the boy lifted and curled with a wolfish malevolence. Like a wolf, he could not long look his father in the eye. His head lowered, and he crumbled to the floor.

"It's Kruger. He . . . he cleaned me out of the money with his slick card playing. He just makes the cards talk in a poker hand. I didn't have no chance with him. When I couldn't pay, he wouldn't hear of waiting. Said . . . said that he'd come gunning for me if I didn't show up with the cash. He gave me till yesterday to get it. I tried cards, I tried everything, even you, to raise the coin. But I couldn't, and I didn't want to kill a man because I owed him money, so I decided to slip out and. . . ."

"You didn't want to kill a man!" cried the sheriff, writhing in his chair with shame and anger. "You didn't want to kill a man! Why, you ran to save your skin, and you know it!"

Jack ground his teeth and flashed one evil glance at the older man. "Nobody else could talk like that," he said, "and you know it. I got to stand it from you. But one of these days. . . ."

"Well?" shouted the sheriff. "One of these days what?"

"You'll be sorry for it," concluded the son lamely. "Now, the point is, what'm I going to do?"

"You're going out and face that rat Kruger without the money and tell him he has to wait for it. That's what you're going to do!"

Jack Clark turned a sickly yellow. "He . . . he's a gunfighter!" he said thickly.

His father was even more yellow of face than he. For a moment he gazed on Jack with unutterable contempt, but then sadness succeeded scorn.

"Yaller," he said at last, "and so yaller that I suppose it must have been born in you just that way. Well, Jack, if you won't fight him, you'll have to run again. But I've made up my mind to one thing. I'm going to make a change with Alison. I'm going right down now and bring her up here and ask her once for all if she wants to marry you. If she says yes . . . all well and good. If she says no, then I won't hold her to it."

Jack Clark burst into a stream of protestation. "Good

Lord," he cried, "ain't she rich? Can't she be the making of both of us? Are you going to throw a whole fortune away because you're a little peeved at me right now?"

"Peeved at you? Well, Jack, you can call it that if you want. But down I go and get her. She's too good for you. I know that. But I'll. . . ."

He said no more but turned and, striding through the office door, he shut it on the clamorous complaints of his offspring. He hurried down the stairs, fearful of letting the good impulse escape before it should have been turned into a concrete fact. But, when he opened the door to the cellar he stopped, his hand freezing to the knob, his whole body shaken with something akin to fear, so great was his wonder—for from the dim shadows of the cellar below him he heard the melody of a girl's laughter.

Chapter Seven

The Sheriff Takes Drastic Action

It must be Alison, and yet—Alison laughing? It was impossible! To be sure, in the old days when her father was alive, she had been a merry little child. But, now that he thought upon it, it was years and years since he had heard her laugh. It was a sufficiently horrible thought, this one that a young girl had not laughed for so long a time that he could not remember, but the sheriff did not dwell on the horror. What chiefly occupied him was wonder at what could have amused her now so heartily.

He slipped a cautious step or two down the stairs and peered below the floor level and through the little forest of upright bars, each faintly marked in place with a sketchy, silver penciling of light from the lantern and from the lamp that Alison had put down. There she was, turned in profile before him, and what an Alison he saw! The fairy godmother had struck her with the wand. The fairy had stripped the drab away and clothed her in sudden beauty. Her fingers were clasped about two bars of The Shifter's cell. She stood with her face close to the bars, her head lifted a little, her eyes bright, the last radiance of the laughter slowly dying from her face. As for The Shifter, he sat on the edge of his bunk with his hands clasped about his knees, teetering slowly back and forth. Certainly he was an amazing young man to sit there so calmly charged with murder.

"But you haven't told me," said Alison, and the quality of her voice was richer and deeper than the sheriff had ever dreamed of hearing from her lips, "you haven't told me why you are here?"

"I'm here," said The Shifter, "because someone disappeared, and they say I'm the cause of it."

Her forehead puckered. Then she started. It was wonderful to the sheriff to see the play of emotion in her. He had known her for so long as having simply a white mask of a face. The chrysalis had been so suddenly broken, and here was a woman before him, young, capable of joy and sorrow, tears and laughter. The sense of her filled the gloomy cellar like a light.

"Does that mean . . . you're accused of . . . ?"

"Yes. But don't say it. It's a hard, black word. It couldn't sound pretty, even from your lips. Well, what are you thinking about? That you shouldn't be down here with a man like me?"

He rose to his feet, more serious than before.

"Oh, no. Of course," she said, and she stretched out her hand toward him with a graceful little gesture of trust. "I know that you are innocent. I know that. I'm only wondering how you can be saved . . . how you can get away."

"By unlocking the door of the cell," he suggested.

"Yes. I think I might be able to get the keys. They're in the sheriff's office."

"And he's the man you're so afraid of?"

"I'd risk it. If it would be any help to you . . . ?"

"No, no!" exclaimed The Shifter. "I won't let you do that! Why, that old devil would make your life a plague. Besides, it wouldn't do me any good."

The sheriff crouched lower against the stairs and gripped his big, bony hands together. It was true. To this youngster he was a veritable devil. He looked at The Shifter with a pang. The makings of a man were in that boy. He had heard enough before of the fighting exploits of The Shifter, and from that last speech he could guess at his generosity and true, quiet courage. Indeed, there were plentiful makings of a man in him, such a man as the sheriff had dreamed once of having in his son. The thought sickened him. He remembered the snarling, shivering man in his office upstairs. Truly, the good angel was close at the side of the sheriff now, pointing out the truth to him.

"Besides," The Shifter was saying, "I'm not going to break away. They can't hang an innocent man. It can't happen. The truth always comes out at the last minute. I've seen it. Looks pretty black for me, I know. I've been tolerable hard. I've done my share and more of fighting. But I'm through with that. I'm going to get out of this mess. Then I'm going to settle down . . . right here in this town, where I've made such a bad start. I'm going to show 'em that I'm all right. I'm going to make 'em like me, just as I've made a pile of others fear me. But making people afraid of you is bad medicine. Look here, you ain't afraid of me, are you?"

"Afraid of you? Why, that's silly!"

"You're a steady one, right enough," said The Shifter, drawing closer to the bars. "You're the sort of stuff a square gent is made of. You'd stick to a friend through thick and thin."

"If I ever found one, of course I would."

"You have no friends?"

"No. They all think I'm queer . . . the people in Vardon City."

"The people in Vardon City are a pile of fools, and I'll show 'em they are! Why, the. . . ." His wrath exploded inwardly, and it made his face a bright red. "I'll tell you what. When I get out of this, d'you know what I'm going to do?"

"Tell me!" said the girl.

How very eager she was, and how close she stood to the bars. The Shifter in turn came close. Their hands were nearing.

"I'm going to get you away from this old scarecrow of a sheriff and take you off where you'll have white folks around you . . . some place where you'll learn to laugh and dance and always have a good time. Understand?"

Her smile was a trifle vague. "I don't know," she said. "I suppose there are such places!"

"Why, right here in Vardon City is such a place. But the point is, would you go with me?"

"Would it be right?"

"I'd make it right!"

"I don't know. I . . . I think I'd have to go, if you asked me to."

"Do you mean that?"

"Yes."

"You'd be happy, then?"

"Oh, don't you see? I've never been happy before, it seems, except just now, talking to you!"

The sheriff saw fire gleam in the eyes of The Shifter, but then the gunfighter drew back a little, drew inside of himself and ground his knuckles across his forehead.

"What's the matter?" she asked tenderly.

"I'm trying to think," he said in a shaking voice. "I'm trying to think what's right for you. That's what comes first. If . . . ?"

The sheriff waited to hear no more. He dragged himself up the stairs and into the hall again, closing the door with trembling fingers. He was so suddenly weak and sick at heart that he slumped against the wall.

Yes, The Shifter was just such a youngster as he had hoped to have in Jack. Honest, clean of mind, clear of eye and heart, brave, kind, reliable. No matter how wild he had been, he would turn out all right. If he took this girl away, he would make her happy as a queen. He would make himself over for her sake. She would have the molding of him. They would work together in the honest partnership which makes a home. *What would become of Jack?* That was the lightning bolt which shattered the dream. What would become of Jack, the gambler, the idler, the shiftless do-nothing? Jack must be saved. How could he be saved? Only through the girl. It was brutally clear to him. She must not be sacrificed. She must not go down!

So the blasting realization grew on him as he climbed the

stairs. His own son—*his own*—was no good. He reached the door of his office. He opened it. Jack was rolling a cigarette with a trembling hand. He started when he saw his father and, as he jumped from the chair, the cigarette was torn to pieces in his fumbling fingers.

The sheriff, as he closed the door, looked over his boy with a glance which for the first time in his life penetrated surely through the exteriors and reached to vital matters inside. He could begin to see the truth, not easily but with a slow and grim grappling. All that he saw made him sick at heart. He himself had made a sad mess of matters, he told himself. He had wasted his money in foolish business ventures. He had done one thing after another wrong in a business sense. But one thing at least could never be said of him. He had never done anything wrong in spirit. In his heart of hearts he had always tried to do right by everyone. The more he thought of this, the more bitter became his insight into the truth of his son. Why had he ever been cursed with such an offspring?

"You're afraid of Kruger?" he said.

"Me? Afraid of him? You see, governor. . . ."

"Don't talk to me!" cried the sheriff in anguish. "Good Lord! A son of mine showing yaller like you're doing . . . well, you've showed it, and that's an end! But I'll tell you this, Jack, you're in worse trouble than you know. If you go down in the village and let folks know that you're alive, and that another gent has been in danger of hanging because of you, you'll get some hard words."

"But I'm not going down into the village," said Jack wildly. "I'm not going to let folks know that I've come back from the pass."

The sheriff started. "You're going to let folks go on thinking that The Shifter killed you?" he asked, repressing his detestation of this man who was his son.

"Why not? What does it matter? Only means that he'll be in jail a couple of days. Anyway, the truth'll come out before he comes to trial. But all I ask is that you don't tell 'em till I get clear of the country. You'll do that, Dad? You won't let 'em know? Kruger would come after me like a hungry dog. And he's a killer . . . a killer!''

He was shuddering with fear as he spoke, and his father shuddered, too, but with a different emotion.

"D'you know what it means to be in a cell under the accusation of murder?"

"I don't know. I don't care. I only know that I got to get clear of this country before Kruger . . . curse him! . . . knows that I'm here."

The sheriff drew a great breath. "What do you intend to do?"

"I'll go up in the hills," said Jack. "I'll take a blanket and a can of beans and go up in the hills. I know where I can find shelter. I'll rest there a day or two. Then I'll strike out."

"You'll leave Vardon City for good?"

"Until you get rid of Kruger."

"I'll never get rid of him. Jack, I've tried you out for a good many years. Listen to me while I talk plain earnest. I've tried you out, and you ain't no good. The Shifter is a real man. Sized up alongside of him, you simply don't count. That's what's opened my eyes. I tell you this . . . you got to get out and stay out. Get out of Vardon City. Get out of my life. I'm through with you. You'd let The Shifter hang, if you could. Well, that opens my eyes to you. Get out and stay out. That's final!"

He turned his back and closed his eyes to the frantic outburst of protestation. He had only one way of closing the mouth of his son. He took out a well-filled wallet and tossed it behind him without looking. Over it he heard Jack whine like a starved dog. Then there was a stream of curses. At length the door closed on the son who was going out of his life.

Chapter Eight
Solicitude Not Wanted

Left to himself, the sheriff stepped to the window and stared into the blackness until he could make out the tops of the trees around the house swinging to and fro in the full current of the wind, for the night had turned wild again, and the storm struck the sides of the house in rattling gusts and then rushed wailing away across the forest. He turned back, shivering, and took down a heavily lined raincoat from the peg. It would be cold outside in that driving blast of rain. He himself was already cold to the heart.

This, however, could be remedied. From a closet he drew forth a brown jug of ample dimensions and, uncorking it, he poured into a water glass a great potion of colorless moonshine. He was normally a very temperate man, but now he drank it off with a toss of the hand and frowned as he felt the alcohol scorch his throat and burn into his vitals.

He was better for it, however. It numbed the thing which was torturing him. It freed his mind. It was even possible to consider the whole affair without heat. The main thing was to undo the wrong to Alison. For that he must have time for thought. Above all, he wanted to be among friends. He buttoned up the raincoat closely beneath his chin, jammed a broad-brimmed sombrero over his ears, and stepped into the hall. The suction of the wind caught the door out of his hand and slammed it with terrific force, so that the floor shook beneath his feet, and the long, desolate echo rang through the lower regions of the house.

Jack must be gone by this time, and the sheriff thought of

204

the boy shrinking when the storm cut against his face. That was the trouble. He had raised Jack too tenderly. If he had the thing to do over again, he would do it differently. Force was the thing—force, force, force! He dinned that thought into his brain every time his heel thudded on the stairs going down to the lower level of the house. There he paused in the hall. A door had opened somewhere in the rear of the house, and a ghost of song had floated toward him, instantly cut off again by the closing of the same door.

It roused a sense of stern revolt in the sheriff. This night of all nights he wanted to hear no music. He strode back down the hall, opened the end door, and listened again, frowning. This time he heard it clearly as the ringing of a far-off bell, every word distinct:

> **What made the ball so fine?**
> **Robin Adair!**
> **What made the assembly shine?**
> **Robin Adair!**

What a voice sang it! A very soul of joy and tenderness was poured into the music, and for a moment the face of the sheriff went blank. Then he rallied, gritting his teeth, and stepped to the kitchen door. When he jerked it open, Alison looked up at him with a dish in one hand and a dishtowel in the other, looked up with the last note dying on her lips and a smile beginning in its place. The heart of the sheriff was touched profoundly.

"Alison . . . ," he began and paused, horror stricken as he realized how much he had taken from this young life—how much a single, short conversation with a condemned man had restored to her. Then he saw that she was waiting patiently, her head obediently bowed—waiting for him to continue his speech. It was the attitude of a slave—the crushed spirit of a slave—and he had done the crushing. "Alison!" he cried,

"I've been wrong! Wrong from the start! Understand that, girl?"

At this she glanced up at him, glanced up with something akin to fear widening her eyes. Plainly she did not understand and, because she did not understand, she was afraid. His thought flashed back to her father, his best friend. Heaven be praised that her father could not see her now!

"What I mean," he continued, making his voice as even as he could, "is that I intend you should be happier, Alison. You need happiness. I've had a wrong idea. I'm going to try to make up to you all the things that I've been wrong in. You understand, honey?"

Her smile was cold and wan. Her nod was one, he could see, of perfunctory acquiescence. "Yes," she said, and her voice had no meaning whatever.

All at once he shrank from her. She was like an incarnation of all his sins. He must escape for more thought. He would go down to the hotel, where the old-timers who knew him would be congregating on this evening of the week. With that thought he rushed out of the house, went to the stables, saddled his horse, led it out, mounted, and rode at a mad gallop down the roadway and into the main street of Vardon City. There he checked the gait to a trot then splashed to a halt under the sheltering roof of the hotel, which projected from the top of the verandah and stretched across an enclosed driving entrance, where a dozen saddle horses and buckboards were already tethered.

He swung down from the stirrup numb of brain and body and, with bent head and sagging stride, he moved slowly up the steps and into the big room which had once been the bar, but where now only soft drinks were dispensed and where the card tables were packed in from wall to wall. There was only a scanty gathering in this social center of the town tonight. But those who had ventured through the whirling wind and the driving rain were hardened old adventurers whom the sheriff had known half his life, men in whom habits had become riveted by long usage. He surveyed their faces for an instant with stern satisfaction. These were men of his own kind. Then he stepped toward the stove and stood before it with his hands extended, until a steam of hot vapor rose from them.

There was a slowly increasing stir among the others. The veterans had greeted him with grunts and nods, after their fashion. Now Bud Morton, still carrying a juvenile nickname through sixty years of hardy action, approached and dropped his hand on the shoulder of the sheriff.

"I sure grieved a pile when I heard what happened," he said. "But what's done is done. Buck up, old man. You still got a long life ahead of you. If it ever comes to a pinch where you need help or a friend, you can call on me." He turned and glanced toward the others. "And here's a dozen more would stand by you, John."

There was a profound hush of sympathy in the room. It was far more eloquent than words. The sheriff could not turn his head. There was only one right answer to this speech and that was to tell them that there was no call for sympathy to be expressed to him. His son was alive and well.

Alive and well! Alive and a self-confessed coward. Far better, indeed, that he should be dead and mourned than that he should be alive and in this condition. He himself—John Clark, known through five states as a fearless man—would rather die than have the shame of his son known, but what could he do? He shrank in all his soul from letting the good men of Vardon City continue to think The Shifter a murderer. Conversely, he dared not proclaim that his son was alive for yonder in the corner he marked the cold, steady eyes of Kruger, the gambler.

In one particular at least Jack had been right. Kruger was a gunfighter. The whole town knew him as such, and the doughty old sheriff would think twice before he invited trouble with the man. He would think twice before he invited trouble, but he would not wait to think even once before he accepted it. That was the difference between himself and his son. That was the difference between courage and cowardice.

He said to Bud Morton, without turning his head: "Thanks, old-timer, thanks!"

Then he scowled down at the stove. How could he explain to them the truth without giving the information to Kruger? Always he felt those cold eyes of the gambler staring at him, probing him from that poker face.

"There's one good thing," said Kruger, "and that's the fact that you got the killer so quick. He'll pay for Jack. He'll pay plenty."

The sheriff raised his head and flashed a glance at Kruger. After all, the man had generous instincts, for otherwise what kept him from telling the sheriff how much was owing to him from his son and demanding payment of the gambling debt, which of all debts is the most sacred? The sheriff remembered how his son had picked up the purse he threw him with a snarl of acknowledgment. What a blind fool he had been to be in ignorance so long as to the real character of the boy.

He must get away from the hotel. These old friends who collected here every week on this day were torture to him. The very fact that he knew them so well was an additional pain. He wanted to be away, aye, in the very midst of the breath and the rain of the storm, so that he could think. He had been an idiot in the first place to come among them.

"Me, too," Bill Culbert was saying. "I've knowed the same thing, partner. I've had my loss, and I've lived through it. Keep your head up, John, and don't figure that this is the end of everything."

Well could Bill Culbert say it. His own son had died a hero's death, saving the lives of men in a mine into which others dared not to go down. Well could Bill Culbert speak, but he, John Clark, was the father of a coward. He turned abruptly.

"Thanks, Bill, old-timer," he said as evenly as he could. "But I'll be riding on. I guess I've had enough of this stove."

He whirled toward the door, strode hastily down the steps, and mounted his horse. Looking through the window, he saw that the men had drawn together, and that they were talking earnestly. No doubt they were talking about his supposed bereavement. Pray heaven that they should never guess at the truth of the matter. He spurred fiercely out into the rain. He must have time and space for thought, and the storm was a fitting accompaniment to the tumult in his brain.

Chapter Nine
A Proposal of Violence

The moment the sheriff's tall form disappeared through the door, the men in the room had been drawn together and called to attention not by any voice from one of their members but by a clarion call from an unexpected quarter. It came from old Nick, the bartender, who smote his hand flatwise upon the bar and cried: "Gents, line up, stand up! What're we going to do for old John Clark?"

They looked at him in surprise and then muttered to one another. What had gotten into placid old Nick? But there he stood with his face lighted, and not pleasantly lighted at that. He was a formidable figure as to chest and stomach and formidable as to hand, also. It was rather fat than brawny now, though there was strength left in it, and many a man—aye, even of those at that moment present—could have testified to the power which once dwelt in that hand in the days of his prime when Nick, disregarding the threat of guns, had more than once stepped in between brawlers and hurled them indiscriminately through the door to roll in the dust outside.

"Fighting is fine for them that likes it," was one of the maxims of Nick, "but my barroom ain't the place for gents to get their exercise and sharpen up their shooting eyes. If you want a roof for gun play, try the sky."

"Gents," he said now when he found that he had successfully focused their attention upon himself, "I've served drinks in a good many towns and worked behind a good many bars in my day. I've done my turn in towns where the gold was coming from the ground so fast that the boys burned their

210

throats out turning the dust into whiskey and getting it down. But I never seen a town act up so plumb orderly and peaceful as Vardon City. That's why I stuck when I come here twenty years ago. And why was it peaceful? They ain't any doubt about why. It was the sheriff. It was old John Clark. Did I have gunfighters smashing up my furniture in here in a way that would have turned the stomach of an honest man that come in here for a quiet drink? I didn't, because the gunfighters was always scarce in Clark's county. Did I have stick-up artists come along and clean out the money box on me? I didn't, because stick-up artists sure hated the ground where John Clark walked. Did I have slick card sharks come along and trim all the boys that played in my place? I didn't, because old John Clark was always a-sitting right over there in the old armchair in the corner . . . that one with the initials carved all over the arms . . . and John could spot a card crook a mile away. Well, boys, it's sure a pleasure to serve drinks in a town that has a sheriff like John Clark, and here's what I'm coming to. For the sake of what he used to do, and for the sake of all the drinks that have spun across this here bar, I sure move that we take a job off Clark's hands and finish up this wild young man-killer, this Shifter as they call him. Are the rest of you with me, or are you not?''

There is an accumulative power in words. They build out of nothing. They lead nowhere. But out of them comes an effect. They have, at least, the value of mass. They have the emphasis of quantity. And the emphasis, in the case of Nick, was pointed by a fierce energy which came out of his heart. Therefore, the effect of his words was more than could have been guessed from a hearing of the words themselves, unbacked by all those connotations which spring out of gesture, tone of voice, flash of eye. In the case of Nick there were tremendous flashes of the eye, great swellings of the chest, convulsive poundings on the bar, polished smooth by the innumerable glasses which in the past twenty years he had slid across its surface.

What, above all, gave the words of the bartender point, was that no one in the crowd had even remotely suspected him of containing in his heart such emotion. When one has jested with a man, shaken his hand, and clapped him upon the shoulder for an indefinite period, it is very difficult to take the same man seriously but, when he actually does become serious, the effect is most astonishing.

The effect was, at least, astonishing now as regarded the old and hardened cattlemen who listened to the eloquence of Nick. First they stared at him; then they gasped at him; and at length they glanced at one another as though to check up their own impressions by the impressions of their neighbors. When they found that their neighbors were taking this fellow seriously, they turned back to Nick with corrugated brows which were in themselves an ample token that they meant business. They began to feel, in short, that John Clark was more than a mere sheriff. He was a representative of the whole population of Vardon City and, as such, he was a representative of each and every man in the town. Each man of those within the room remembered how many times in the past the sheriff had stood by him in such and such an emergency. Each and every man was, in his heart, a little ashamed to think that the veteran bartender had outdone him in loyalty to the guardian of the law.

Shame, then, was the bellows from which air was blown upon the fire, and shame is a power well worth taking into consideration. Too few are those who think upon it seriously, but shame is that thing which makes the soldier step out before his mates and dare the impossible. Shame is the spur which the bright spirit doth raise. Indeed, even the stern Milton would probably nod his head in agreement to the misquotation of his great line. At least, it operated powerfully upon the good men of Vardon City, although there was some argument on the head.

"Speaking personal," said Bud Morton, shaking his gray head from side to side as he spoke, "I always figured that Jack Clark was no more like his father than a half-blood colt of a mustang mare is like a Thoroughbred sire. He's mean by nature, a sneak by training, and a hound by general principles.''

Harry Peyton came to the rescue of the Clark family and particularly of its son. "Look at most youngsters," he said, "and, if you look close enough, you'll find that, no matter how well they mean, they ain't no good in practice."

"Now you're talking wise," said Morton. "Anybody here can step out and say that I'm the sheriff's friend. I've proved it with powder and lead, which out-talks words a good many ways, but I'm also here to state that, no matter how much I like the sheriff, I ain't overfond of his son. If the rest of you would dig down into your vitals and talk true, I think you'd say the same.

"I've seen him quiet, and I've seen him loud. I've seen him talking friendly, and I've seen him talking mean. I'm cussed if I ever seen him talk or act the way I like to see a man. He always made me figure that he was only one part a man. At that, I've always give him the best part of the guess. I've always tried to see his father in him. But I ain't never been able to see much of John Clark in Jack Clark. Them two don't seem to string together.

"Why are we figuring to hit this gent they call The Shifter? We figure to go after him because he met Jack Clark on the one-way trail. What are the facts? The facts are that The Shifter was going the right way, and Jack Clark was riding the wrong way on the one-way trail. Well, boys, work it out for yourselves. It ain't hard to do. Suppose you or me was to meet a gent riding the wrong way on a trail when they wasn't room for two gents to pass. What would we do? I ask you that. What would we do? Why, we'd simply up with a gun and get rid of the gent that was superfluous. And this ain't the first time, because there's Hugh Neer. Didn't Hugh Neer take the wrong way of the trail, and didn't he get shot by Billy Jordan, and didn't Billy come into town and boast about what he done, and didn't all of us shake Billy's hand? I ask you that?''

It was a long speech to be made in the name of a defendant not present. Certainly, had The Shifter known of it, he should have presented his thanks to Bud Morton. But as it was, The Shifter was thinking of far, far other things than speeches made in his defense. In fact, he was clinging confidently to a doctrine absurdly old and that doctrine held no man could be lost for a crime which he had not committed.

However, there is no argument so old that it will not meet with a refutation; there is no argument so old that it will not draw out an enemy; there is no argument so strong that some-one will not take the opposite side. This is human nature. We delight in opposition. We plague our dearest friends with epigrams. So it was in the present instance. There arose from the ranks of the crowd one who was willing to stake his wits against the wits of all the others, not because he felt that he was inherently right, but simply because he desired to fight the great majority. This is the impulse which drives men to support lost causes. What wonder that it showed itself here, in the person of the gray and venerable Jefferson Smith?

Jefferson Smith was, so to speak, a tartar. In other words, he generally did the opposite of what people expected. Because he was the opposite of their expectations, it is not strange to hear that he was generally detested. What we hate is not, as a rule, what is dangerous to us, but what is new to us. So, to speak plainly, Jefferson Smith was quite generally hated. He was so generally hated that good wives, if one must be perfectly frank, dreaded his shadow over their doorway. He was so generally hated that men cared not at all if their secrets fell into the hands of the ordinary run of mortals, but they cared extremely much if those secrets fell into the hands of Jefferson Smith. Because Jefferson Smith was able to impart to the smallest thing that aroma of the important which may not exist in fact but which is very apt to exist in inference. He was one of those men whose inferences are more important than their statements.

It was this Jefferson Smith, then, who rose in what had been the ancient and respected barroom of the hotel at Vardon City. He rose and looked about him, and by his very rising he called to him the eyes and the attention of the spectators. They turned on their heels, they turned in their chairs, and they beheld Jefferson Smith rise and roll his eyes and tug at his slender beard, for it is not for nothing that in the West a man has shot a five-cent piece at thirty yards and blown its center out. It is not for nothing, either, that a man has killed three hard-fighting warriors of Colt forty-five and bronco. So every man in the old barroom of the hotel turned himself toward Jefferson Smith and watched him with the eye of one intent.

Which side would Jefferson take? Both were fairly represented. If not, every one knew that he would throw himself with the minority. It was generally conceded that by his weight he could determine the whole affair—the life or death of The Shifter was dependent upon the careless malignity or the careless generosity of this fiery old fellow. He allowed them to remain in the dark about his intentions for only a short time.

"Gents," he said, "it seems to me that we're all wasting a pile of valuable time about a mighty small thing. Are all of us going to stand around here and spend the night chattering about a youngster like The Shifter? Bah! I've heard of him. We all have. We've heard him talked about as a man-killer . . . a bad one." Jefferson turned his eye deliberately over the little crowd, and deliberately he picked out his two worst enemies. "Gimme Calkins and Bud Morton to stand with me, and the three of us will take on thirty of such half-baked badmen. I say, boys, that we ought to ride up the hill to Clark's place, take this Shifter out of his cell, string him up to the highest tree we can find, and leave him there flapping in the breeze as a sign to others of what Vardon City does to the badmen who come its way."

He pointed his speech with action as he stepped toward the door. "Who's coming with me?" he said. "Or do you want me to go alone?" And that was decisive.

Chapter Ten
Alison Acts

Alison had not gone to bed. She sat with her face so close to the window in her room that sometimes the pane pressed cold against her nose. Beyond the glass, as her eyes grew accustomed to the night, she could make out vague outlines here and there. Sometimes the sheeted rain was an effective curtain that fenced away the rest of the world. Sometimes it shook away in a change of the wind, and she saw the looming forest. Whatever she saw was noted only in semi-consciousness. Her mind was busy, terribly busy, with the host of thoughts that had been crammed into it this day.

The Shifter—Harry French—was a gunfighter, a known badman. It seemed impossible that this could be the case, but then she was sadly ignorant of men. It might be that she liked him so much simply because he was the opposite of Clark and his son. She admitted this to herself, nodding her head wisely but very sick at heart. She admitted it to her reason, but reason did not satisfy her. If The Shifter were really bad, then she felt that there was no such thing as goodness in the world. The very sound of his voice thrilled her with happiness; the very memory of it was a joy.

"But I don't know much about things," she said to herself aloud. "Most likely I'm wrong, because I don't know much about men."

She had not entirely obeyed the command of her guardian to keep away from The Shifter. She had stolen down into the cellar after she had finished with the dishes, and The Shifter had risen with a smile to greet her.

"Somebody's been talking to you, I guess," he said bitterly when she shrank away from him, watching with frightened eyes. "Somebody's been telling you that I'm a regular snake, eh? Full of poison?"

"I only wanted to know," she answered, "if you'd like to have some books or magazines to read?"

"I'd rather have you to talk to," answered The Shifter at once. "You're a pile better than all the books in the world."

She retreated a little, and yet instinct was singing in her that there was nothing to fear in this man—nothing at all to fear.

"All right," he called gloomily, "if you're going to believe 'em, go ahead and stay away. I'll manage somehow. Good night."

She could not muster courage to answer him. Something was choking her. So she turned and, once her back was toward him, a cold panic sent her scurrying up the steps and through the hall and up again to her room. Here she had been crouched beside the window ever since, harried back and forth by thoughts of The Shifter and his bright, steady blue eyes. She could visualize him so keenly that the eyes of the vision became intolerantly bright and brought her heart up into her throat.

It was at this point that she heard the sound of the knocking at the front door. The sound came dimly up the stairs through the clamoring of the storm. Perhaps the sheriff had forgotten his key. The thought of the sheriff in a passion was quite sufficient to blot all other considerations from her mind. She fled down the stairs like a deer and, panting, pulled open the front door against the drag and suction of the wind. Then the draft nearly drew her out into the night but, as she balanced on tiptoe, she made out that on the porch was not a single figure but a whole group of bewhiskered men glistening faintly through the night in their wet slickers.

"It's the girl," said one voice. "I'd forgot about her. It's the girl. That makes it bad!"

"Who are you?" she asked. "Uncle John is not here. I think you'll find him in the hotel."

Instead of answering, one of the men pushed in. He was a little man, not as tall as she, in fact. He had a sharply pointed little gray beard and glittering little gray eyes. He was withered with the passage of sixty years or more, but he had dried up without growing feeble. He was weather brown. His wrinkled skin looked as tough as leather. His active, gleaming eyes filled her with dread just as she trembled when the eyes of a rat glittered out of a shadowy corner at her. He stared through and through her. He seemed to be poking into veiled corners of her nature. There was nothing that could be hidden from this terrible little man.

Others came in behind him. Some of them were big, all of them were quite old, and all of them had brows wrinkled with knowledge of the world and its men and women and events. The silence with which they trooped in was strange and rather terrible. Alison shrank back toward the wall.

"You can come in, of course," she said. "I'll build a fire for you in the front room . . . and make you some coffee. You must be terribly cold . . . and wet!"

The little man turned toward the others.

"I'll handle this," he said.

Then he turned back to Alison and laid his hand on her shoulder. His voice was smooth and kind. It was wonderful to hear. It sent a drowsy sense of security drifting through her. The hand on her shoulder was light as the touch of an affectionate child.

"Now don't you go bothering about us, honey," he said. "Don't you go bothering to fix up coffee. We'll get along without that. Thing for you to do is just to trot back up to your room and go to bed. We know the sheriff ain't here. But we've come to do something that he'll be glad to have done. We're all old friends of his . . . you see?"

He patted her shoulder lightly as he spoke, and yet it seemed to the sensitive eyes of the girl that there was no reality in his smile. He was not talking to her but around her, just as the sheriff often talked when he wished to keep his true meaning from her. Being a specialist, as one might say, in pain, she recognized the same tactics in Jefferson Smith. The claws were buried not so very deeply beneath the velvet. Yet behind her own blank gaze the wise little man was not able to penetrate to the hidden meanings. She seemed to him perfectly simple, and he gave a little more credence than he ever had before to the tale which the sheriff had spread throughout Vardon City that the mind of the girl was weak. For that very reason he was tenderer and gentler with her.

The other men stepped quietly into the hall and closed the door softly behind them. It embarrassed them hugely to find only this reputedly weak-minded girl as a garrison in the sheriff's house. It was like attacking a helpless woman in a way. They scowled fiercely at one another, those hardy old veterans of the frontier. It would be better to have the sheriff himself present to overmaster and bind before they went after his prisoner.

In the meantime, Jefferson Smith continued to engineer the affair as general of the party. "I'll go upstairs with you," he said. "You can show me the sheriff's office. Can you do that?"

She nodded and turned, passing slowly and with bent head up the stairs, for she was deeply in thought. She knew it was by no means ordinary for a group of men to call in the absence of John Clark and calmly ask to be shown into his office. That office was his sanctum. He hardly allowed Jack, his own son, to step inside those precincts.

What was up? In the guilty, storm-reddened faces of the men she had striven in vain to read the secret. But undeniably there was something fierce behind their attitude, something in the eye of Jefferson Smith which reminded her forcefully of the eye of a cat that sits patiently at the hole of the mouse with steel-like claws ready to strike inescapably. She showed her guest to the door of the sheriff's office.

He paused there with his hand on the knob. "All right, honey. Now you run along to bed. Good night. And happy dreams!"

She looked wistfully up into his face. In spite of his smiling lips, his forehead remained stern. What was going on inside his mind? But all she could do was nod slowly and then turn away down the hall as Smith entered the room. However, she had hardly taken a step when, immediately after the sound of the scratching match and the small flurry of light in the office, she heard the jingle of metal against metal, the unmistakable sound of keys knocking together.

It brought Alison whirling back to the door with her heart a-flutter, for those keys, she knew, were the keys to the prison in the cellar—and there was only one reason for wanting those keys, which was to get at the prisoner—to get at The Shifter. And there, through the partly opened door, she saw Jefferson Smith turning away from the desk with the big, shining bundle of keys in his hand, and on his face an expression of cold and sinister purpose.

The mind of the girl leaped at once to the result. She had heard of lynchings. The absence of the sheriff gave point to her flash of suspicion. She reached in, drew the door to her. Cautiously slipping the key from the lock, she fitted it again on the outside and noiselessly shut the door and turned the lock.

So softly had she worked that Smith, half blinded by the flare of the match close to his eyes, was not suspicious. "House full of drafts," she heard him mutter as he reached the door on the inside. Then came the sound of the turning knob.

There was such a terror in her, now that she had acted, that she could not move but leaned half fainting against the wall of the hall.

"Hello!" she heard Jefferson Smith cry. "What the devil has . . . ?" He wrenched loudly at the door. "Hello! Help!"

he shouted aloud. "Hey, boys, the little vixen has tricked me and locked me up here like a rat in a trap."

That brought her to her senses. The shouting of the storm still was louder than the voice of Smith, and there was no rush of footsteps from the lower part of the house, but at any moment it might begin. She turned and fled down the hall.

Chapter Eleven
The Escape

Her mind was working with singular precision now. She raced down the back stairs to the tool room behind the kitchen and there, with swift and sure touch, she jerked open the big tool chest in the corner and drew out the steel saw and the oil can. More than once she had seen the sheriff work with it, more than once she had seen him handle stout iron.

Thus equipped, she hurried down to the hall, slipped through the cellar door, and paused a moment before she closed it. There was a sudden outbreak of shouting in the front part of the house. Then came a roar of footfalls on the front stairs. They had heard Jefferson Smith, and they were rushing to his rescue. *How long would the locked door hold them at bay?* she thought, as she tossed the key down the steps.

She ran straight to the cell. The lantern now illumined the big room very faintly, for it was turned low. The Shifter, lying asleep on his cot, was a blotchy shadow among shadows. The girl pressed her face against the cold bars. Her voice shook crazily as she called, and yet she dared not call too loudly.

"Quick! Quick! They've come for you! Wake up!"

The fear in her voice seemed to reach him even in his sleep. One bound brought him to his feet, staring wild eyed at her.

"They've come!" she stammered. "Here . . . here's the saw. I'll put on the oil . . . !"

"Who's come?"

"Jefferson Smith and a lot of others . . . hard-faced men . . . and they mean to take you away. They've taken the keys in the sheriff's office and. . . ."

She watched his eyes widen, his face turn gray.

"A lynching party!" breathed The Shifter. "Good Lord!"

The saw was snatched from her hand and began its small, shrill song as it cut into the steel bar, until she silenced it with a trickle of oil from the can.

"Hurry!" she pleaded. "Hurry!"

Remembering a vital step which had not been taken, she rushed back to the cellar door and opened it an instant, barely in time to hear a great tearing and crashing sound in the upper part of the house, as though the storm had beaten in a section of the roof. On its heels came a shout of triumph.

They had broken down the door to the sheriff's office with their combined shoulder weight. With palsied hands she closed and locked the cellar door and blessed its solid thickness of stout pine wood as she did so. Then she fled down the steps again and back to The Shifter.

He was working like mad, his face covered with tiny beads of perspiration but absolutely without color, and he acknowledged her return with a frantic rolling of the eyes. Again she picked up the oil can and poured the trickle on the shimmering blade of the saw. It was eating into the heart of the steel bar, but how slowly, slowly, slowly.

"Quick!" she sobbed. "I hear them coming!"

An instant later the body of a man crashed against the cellar door. The Shifter cast the saw jangling on the floor and grasped the bar. It held as though it were a column of stone. The guarding door which kept out the manhunters groaned as they assailed it again. A gun exploded. They were shooting through the lock, but that massive, old-fashioned lock would surely turn their bullets without giving way.

"Once more," cried Alison and, laying hold on the bar, she added her own small strength now made large in her frenzy.

He gripped the bar again. All his strength of body, from head to heel, went into the effort. There was a slight bending, then a gritting sound as of crystal against crystal, and suddenly the bar snapped with a humming sound and bent far to the side. The Shifter flung himself headlong into the gap. He could not go through at once. In fact, his struggles as he was pinned there threatened to tear him to pieces, but finally his hips were through, and then he lay sprawling on the floor at her feet, while at the same instant the cellar door was burst from its hinges and went crashing and bounding down the steps with a flood of yelling men pouring through behind it.

"Get him!" yelled the shrill voice of Jefferson Smith. "Shoot to kill, boys. He's loose!"

She saw a flash of fighting rage come into the eyes of The Shifter. Then he caught up the fallen saw and flung it at the lantern which hung from the rafter a few yards away. The lantern fell crashing, and the big cellar was filled with sudden, thick darkness.

In that darkness she heard the pursuers bang blindly into the bars and shout and curse furiously. Then a hand gripped her.

"Is there another way out? Is there another way beside the one back into the house?"

"Yes . . . yes. If I can only find it in the darkness! Oh, heaven help us!" sobbed Alison.

Deftly she guided him down the alley through the cells and then sharply to the right, until they ran into the rear wall of the house. The hubbub continued in the front of the room, a babel of oaths and frantic callings for a light. Here and there a match glowed, cupped in big hands, but those feeble cups of light were not able to throw a ray into the far corner where Alison fumbled for the old door.

At least, there was a sufficient glimmer of light for her to see that the way was blocked with a big box, and she pointed it out to the prisoner. His hands were instantly on it. It was flung to the side, while the betraying sound brought a yell from the trailers. One thrust of his shoulder and the door went open. Then she stood with him in the freshness of the night, with the wild rain whipping about them.

"Which way?" he asked.

"Here!"

She barely gave him the signal when he was off and she, racing beside him, was able to keep up because of her knowledge of the ground. Twice he tripped and fell headlong over obstacles in the yard and so enabled her to stay near him, and they reached the sheltering darkness of the trees side by side behind the house. The noise of the self-appointed posse now burst out of the cellar and into the storm-ridden night.

"Go back and get lights!" shouted the controlling voice of Jefferson Smith. "We'll run the fool down. He can't get far on foot. Newt Barclay and Saunders, run for the stable and see that he don't get off with a hoss. If you see anything, don't wait to ask questions. Shoot to kill. Jerry, wait here and watch this door so he don't double back like a fox. The rest of you. . . ." His voice died away as he turned back into the cellar.

"Now," said The Shifter grimly to the girl, "you've sure done your share. You've given me a running start, and I'll do the rest of it. Go back to the house."

"Go back and face the sheriff? Oh, I'd sooner die. You don't know him. He'll kill me for this!"

"Is he that kind? But, you can't go with me."

"Shall I go alone, then? I know the ground. I can show you where to go . . . a place they'll never search for you. Only one other person in the world knows about it. And . . . I won't be much in you way. I'll run every step!"

"Lord bless you," said The Shifter. "In the way? After saving me? I'll keep you in spite of everything. If I only had a gun . . . if I only had a measly little Twenty-Two. But bare hands are better than nothing. Which way, then?"

"Follow me."

She led straight through the heart of the trees, keeping her word valiantly and running ahead over the slippery ground with a sureness of foot and a strength that amazed The Shifter. It was all he could do to keep close to the form which twinkled back and forth as she raced through the trees. In a moment more they came to a stiff upgrade with the trees growing in a more scattered fashion.

"Now we're fairly started," she panted, slowing to a walk. "They'll never catch us before we reach the place."

A gust of wind pitched her into his arms, and he held her close for a moment then whipped off his coat and wrapped it around her shoulders, for her thin house dress was already soaked from the rainfall.

"Come on," said The Shifter. "If they follow us, heaven help the ones I lay my hands on!"

Chapter Twelve
New Lives

They labored up a weary climb, their feet slipping on the muddy slope, but never once did the courage or the spirit of the girl fail her, so that The Shifter was struck with wonder again and again.

"It's a short cut," she told him. "They'll never dream of coming this way, and the best of it is that the rain will wash out our footmarks. They won't last till the morning."

"And what of you?" he asked. "What will you do, Alison? Are you going to give up your home?"

"It's not a home," she said. "It's a prison. Oh, if you knew how I love even the rain and the wind because I'm free at last! My whole soul is breaking out and growing bigger. I feel strange to myself, I'm so happy. And I...." She stopped suddenly and caught at his arm. "Listen!"

"Well?"

"Do you hear a wailing?"

"It's the wind. Yes, I hear it."

"No, no. Not the wind. I've heard it before. I heard it when the jail break came last spring, and the two men got away. Jefferson Smith has got out his hounds! Listen again!"

He could catch it unmistakably now, for as she spoke the force of the wind fell away a little, the crash of the rain on the rocks was lighter, and the chorus of the deep-throated bloodhounds swelled heavily up the hillside.

"We're almost there!" she sobbed. "But what good will it do to go into the cave? They'll follow us even there!"

"Will the scent hold in all this rain?"

"Uncle John says that the Smith dogs can follow even the thought of a man. Yes, the scent will hold for them!"

"If we're near the cave, then," said The Shifter, "let's go there and sit down a minute to think. My head's in a whirl in this infernal wind. Come on!"

He helped her up an almost precipitous rise of ground, digging his toes deep into the mud for footing. They came onto a little shelf of land on the mountainside.

"This is it," said Alison. "At least this cave will give us a cut-off and gain time. It passes clear through the hill and opens on the other side."

"Suppose we cut through it and then block the other end with stones. The hounds may be thrown off."

"Yes, yes! At least we can try."

She led the way, dropping to her hands and knees and crawling through the black mouth of the cave. The Shifter followed and found himself in pitchy darkness. For perhaps twenty feet he crawled on behind the girl, bumping his head when he attempted to straighten. But at length he was able to see her rise to her feet, and he followed her example. The cave had widened to comfortable dimensions. The smell of wet ground was thick around them mixed with another scent, fainter and sharper.

"Alison!" exclaimed The Shifter softly. "There's someone else here! I smell wood smoke. A fire has been burning in the cave."

"That can't be true," she answered instantly. "There's only one other person in the world who knows about it, and that's poor Jack. He and I used to come up here when we were little ones. Jack showed it to me. The wood smoke may have drifted up here and stayed here without being blown out."

"But . . . ?"

He checked himself. There was no time to worry about imaginary dangers, for the voices of the bloodhounds swelled faintly from beyond. The Shifter struck on again through the cave, bending far over to avoid striking his head against any projection. For some ten yards the passage held straight on. Then it veered sharply to the right, and The Shifter, striding blindly ahead, struck solidly against the rock wall.

He recoiled with an exclamation, and on the sound of his voice he was paralyzed with astonishment to have a broad shaft of light flashed upon him.

"Hands up!" snapped a voice. "Hands up, whoever you are!"

The Shifter obeyed.

"If you're hiding out here, partner," he said eagerly, "I'm not hunting you. Matter of fact, I'm in the same boat. And. . . ."

"You!" broke in the holder of the electric torch, and now The Shifter could make out the outlines of the figure and even the glimmer of the revolver which he held in his right hand as he poised the electric torch in the left. "I figured I'd meet you again. But I never dreamed I'd get a chance to get back at you so quick. Now, son, you'll pay me for my hoss you killed, and you'll pay me big!" He added sharply: "Who's that with you?"

"Jack!" cried Alison, her voice ringing out joyously. "Oh, then all the danger is over! Don't you see? It's Jack Clark. He's not dead . . . he's not dead!"

"Good Lord!" groaned Jack, the torch wavering in his hand as he recoiled. "Alison, what're you doing up here . . . with him? What're you doing up here?"

The mind of The Shifter groped vaguely toward the truth. Here was the "murdered" man, after all, safe and sound and lurking like a condemned criminal escaped from the law.

"You'd've hung up here?" he growled savagely. "Stayed right up here while they was holding me for killing you? Clark, you'll pay *me* big for this."

"Will I? And suppose I stop your trail right now? If I catch you running off with a girl, d'you s'pose I ain't got the right to stop you . . . with a bullet?"

The Shifter had been resting one hand against the rocky side of the passage. Now in his blind rage his fingers contracted strongly, and a great chunk of stone came away in them. All caution left him.

"You hound!" he cried and lurched straight at the holder of the light.

The sound of the explosion of the revolver and the mingling wail of the girl rolled faintly out from the cave and reached the spurring horsemen who were driving their exhausted mounts up that hillside on the heels of the dogs, held hard in leash by Jefferson Smith and giving tongue furiously as the scent grew hot.

Up to the very mouth of the cave the hounds dragged Smith. He pulled them to one side, and the others crawled into the black hole. The scent of burned gun powder was lingering inside to guide them. Far away they heard the muffled weeping of a woman. Morton had found an electric pocket lantern before he left the sheriff's house, and with this he now probed the passage with a dim shaft of light. They turned the corner of the tunnel at a run and so came full upon a strange group.

A man lay sprawled on his face, motionless. Another stood above him, leaning against the wall and staring stupidly down at the stricken. And Alison crouched, weeping, nearby.

"It's me," said The Shifter slowly as they rushed about him. "He tried to shoot me. I hit him with this rock. And . . . and I think this time you got some call to hang me, boys."

Bud Morton turned the fallen man on his back, and a shout of astonishment rose from his lips as he saw the face of Jack Clark. It was a face half muddy and half pale, and from the side of the head a trickle of crimson ran down his face.

"Is he dead?" asked Jefferson Smith from the rear.

"No," answered Morton, his hand lying over Jack's heart.

"He'd better be," said Jefferson in a ringing voice. "Of all the dirty pieces of work I've ever seen or heard of, boys, this is the rottenest. Don't you see it? To get square with The Shifter there, who killed his hoss and maybe licked him fair and square on the one-way trail, this skunk waited up here till

The Shifter swung for the job or got lynched. Lynch The Shifter? Why, boys, we'll step up and tell him we're a pile sorry for what's happened.''

It required time to bring about the conclusion. In that time Jack Clark, a sadly humbled and humiliated man, went north, far north into a new country, to carve out for himself a new name and a new character. And, since there is possibility of change in even the worst of us, Jack succeeded beyond the dreams of even his father who went with him. There in the north they settled down as farmers in an unknown community, and the letters that drifted south to Alison were all of prosperity, home building, and finally of the marriage of Jack.

They will tell you the story even today in Vardon City, particularly when a stranger is guided through the main street and past the big house at the head of the thoroughfare, its gables barely visible above the surrounding treetops, for Harry French, late The Shifter, and his wife now live in the big house. Their greatest friend is that formidable gunfighter, Jefferson Smith, who takes all the credit for their romance on his own shoulders.

"I smelled a rat from the first," he is fond of saying. "And then I ran it down with dogs. No matter if the name of the rat was not the one I started after. The fact is that I found a rat."

No one cares to dispute Jefferson Smith. Certainly not The Shifter who has laid aside his guns.

About the Author

Max Brand is the best-known pen name of Frederick Faust, creator of Dr. Kildare, Destry, and many other fictional characters popular with readers and viewers worldwide. Faust wrote for a variety of audiences in many genres. His enormous output, totaling approximately thirty million words or the equivalent of five hundred and thirty ordinary books, covered nearly every field: crime, fantasy, historical romance, espionage, Westerns, science fiction, adventure, animal stories, love, war, and fashionable society, big business and big medicine. Eighty motion pictures have been based on his work along with many radio and television programs. For good measure he also published four volumes of poetry. Perhaps no other author has reached more people in more different ways.

Born in Seattle in 1892, orphaned early, Faust grew up in the rural San Joaquin Valley of California. At Berkeley he became a student rebel and one-man literary movement, contributing prodigiously to all campus publications. Denied a degree because of unconventional conduct, he embarked on a series of adventures culminating in New York City where, after a period of near starvation, he received simultaneous recognition as a serious poet and successful popular-prose writer. Later, he traveled widely, making his home in New York, then in Florence, and finally in Los Angeles.

Once the United States entered the Second World War, Faust abandoned his lucrative writing career and his work as a screenwriter to serve as a war correspondent with the infantry in Italy, despite his fifty-one years and a bad heart. He was killed during a night attack on a hilltop village held by the German army. New books based on magazine serials or unpublished manuscripts or restored versions continue to appear so that, alive or dead, he has averaged a new book every four months for seventy-five years. In the United States alone nine publishers now issue his work. Beyond this, some work by him is newly reprinted every week of every year in one or another format somewhere in the world. Yet, only recently have the full dimensions of this extraordinarily versatile and prolific writer come to be recognized and his stature as a protean literary figure in the twentieth-century acknowledged. His popularity continues to grow throughout the world.

"Max Brand is a topnotcher!"
—*The New York Times*

King Charlie. Lord of sagebrush and saddle leather, leader of outlaws and renegades, Charlie rules the wild territory with a fist of iron. But the times are changing, the land is being tamed, and men like Charlie are quickly fading into legend. Before his empire disappears into the sunset, Charlie swears he'll pass his legacy on to only one man: the ornery cuss who can claim it with bullets—or blood.
__4182-0 $4.50 US/$5.50 CAN

Red Devil of the Range. Only two things in this world are worth a damn to young Ever Winton—his Uncle Clay and the mighty Red Pacer, the wildest, most untamable piece of horseflesh in the West. Then in one black hour they are both gone—and Ever knows he has to get them both back. He'll do whatever it takes, even if it costs his life—or somebody else's.
__4122-7 $4.50 US/$5.50 CAN